The Janus House

By

Richard How

Prologue

Have you ever wondered if the world around you is actually real?

My name is Francis Smith; I think; I am no longer sure. I have recently lost a grip on what I think is real. I know people call me by that name but I am full of doubt; I no longer trust my senses. The words of the distant philosophers echo in my head. Are my senses deceiving me? How can I be certain that my life is not a dream? Reality for me has become a bit blurred. It is why my counsellor, has asked me to write down what I know. I did tell him that what I know and what is may not be the same but he was insistent; so I agreed to give it a go. If I ramble a little you will have to excuse me; my mind is not what it used to be; the solid foundations that I built my life on are no longer there.

To start with, and so that you understand how I have come to reach this point, I must explain those 'solid foundations'. The things I thought were correct in my life not so long ago; for instance, the fact that I am thirty five years old, that I grew up in a small village in England, a healthy, proud, young person ready to take on the world. My parents loved me and doted on me. I went to church every week and felt that God was always on my side. I followed the expected pathway without thought or challenge. I went to university, got a good job; I married a beautiful girl and have two lovely children. We live in a nice, suburb on the edge of a rural town. The house is modern, chaotic as any place is with two young children and two working parents.

This gets me to the point where my story really begins; a few months before last Christmas when I met Geoff.

I

'Right I'm off now Rosie' I said as I picked up my work bag and headed for the door 'I need to be in early today. Are you two ready yet? You'll miss your bus.'

'Yes dad,' Theresa and Michael replied in unison, neither of them actually looking very ready and neither of them moving from the settee where they were watching the morning television, their breakfast plates and cups scattered on the floor around them with their school things.

'O.K., have a good day at school both of you.' I turned and shouted up the stairs 'Bye love!' then headed out of the door.

I liked to arrive at the office early. It was a good chance to catch up on paperwork and prepare for the day ahead before it got too busy to concentrate but this morning I was not the first in. Sitting in the far corner was a man that I had hardly noticed before. It was a big open office, which usually buzzed with people coming and going.

'Hello' I said as I walked past. Getting no reply, I turned. The man, who was about my age, looked crumpled, unshaven. His eyes were red. He looked as though he was not used to getting much sleep. 'You okay?' He looked up.

'What?' He mumbled, not really taking me in.

'You okay?' I repeated.

'Oh yes I suppose so' he replied not very convincingly.

'You don't look so good.' I said feeling a bit of a Good Samaritan. 'Do you want a coffee?' He looked at me with a leave me alone stare which made me more determined. 'It's no trouble I'm having one. How do you like it?'

'Um, I don't ….' I was already walking over to our small kitchen. I soon had two mugs of coffee. I poked my head out of the kitchen. The man was sitting looking at the desk, his head in his hands. He looked up at me, his face a picture of confusion and despair.

'Milk? Sugar?'

'Err, yes please. Two sugars.' I put in two large sugars, feeling he needed the energy and carried the mugs across, handing him one.

'Thanks.'

No problem. I'm Francis. Don't think we've met.'

'Err no. I'm Geoff. I tend to keep to myself…' he began to mumble. It sounded to me like he said 'It's safer that way.' But I could not be sure and did not want to push him. I felt an urge just to leave him and get on with the pressing work that I had come in to do, but I was intrigued, as we all are by other peoples' pain and suffering. Now the Good Samaritan had left me and I just wanted to know.

It is something innate within us that means we want to know other people's business. Perhaps this is just so that we can gossip about it later or perhaps it is so we can live our lives through others to make up for the inadequacies that we perceive in our own, or is it just to relieve the boredom that is everyday living, an attempt to find something more.

But no matter how hard I tried I could not draw him out. He just sipped his coffee and looked at his desk, refusing to make eye contact. In the end the need to get on with my work won me over and I left him feeling as though I had absorbed some of his depression and sat gloomily at my desk.

It was a month before I next spoke to Geoff. I mean actually spoke to him. I would see him most days and say hello but he would always mutter an excuse and leave. He looked rough when I first saw him but somehow each day he became more decrepit.

The office was organising a get together at a local pub. Lola and Abigail, the chief instigators of all our get-together's, were discussing the plans in the kitchen as I made a cup of tea.

'You going to invite Geoff?' I asked.

'Everyone's invited. It is an office get together after all Francis.'

'He never goes though does he? I hadn't even noticed him in the office before until the other day.'

Who is Geoff?' said Abigail. I pointed to him through the door. 'Oh him; he's so quiet I've never took much notice of him. He always looks so sad.'

'He's never attended anything before from what I can remember' said Lola. 'But feel free to try to talk him into it. It'd do him some good to get out.'

Do you know anything about him?' I asked her feeling that if anyone was going to know him it would be the office gossip.

'No he just appeared one day sat down and started work. I've tried to chat to him but he never really responds. He's got a beautiful wife apparently; although you wouldn't believe it to look at him.'

'Marital problems I bet.' chipped in Abigail. 'That'll explain the hound dog look.'

'Go on then ask him. It's Friday after work at The Plume. Bet you, you can't get him to come.'

'Err O.K.' I felt I had backed myself into a corner on this one. So I headed uncertainly across to Geoff. The two girls watched me from the kitchen door.

'Hi Geoff,' I sat down on a spare seat by his desk.

'Hello Francis.' He looked at me nervously.

'Are you interested in going out for a drink after work on Friday?'

'No' he replied quickly 'My wife, she expects me back...' he mumbled by way of an explanation.

'Oh come on. It's just one night. Besides if you don't I'm going to have to buy the drinks. The girls have bet me I can't get you to come.' He looked up at them. They smiled across at us. He turned his gaze upon me. I felt his eyes drilling into me.

'You shouldn't invite me. It'll end badly.' His face seemed so serious it worried me.

'Oh don't be silly' I said trying to disperse the tension. 'It's only for a drink what harm can that do? We all feel we don't know you very well and it will give us a chance to chat.' I continued feeling my misgivings growing. I could see he did not know what to do and could not think of a way out of it. I felt bad pushing him into a corner and realised I was only doing it because the two girls were watching me. I could see something was holding him back but at the same time he did not want to say no. He was a lonely man and he was being given an opportunity to share some of his burdens. It looked as though he wanted that but did not know if he had the courage to do it. 'Hey look I don't want to put pressure on you.' I relented feeling guilty. 'Tell us tomorrow if you want to come.' He smiled with some relief.

'Okay.'

Early the next morning Geoff and I were the only ones in the office.

'Morning Geoff decided whether you want to come along tomorrow evening.' He looked up at me distraught.

'You know the trouble is I really would like to come. I have not been out for so long.' He looked at me calculating. It made the hairs on the back of my neck stand up. Suddenly I had a rush of concern. I was not sure why and quickly tried to put it out of my mind. 'I know I shouldn't go.' He continued 'and I give you the chance now before anything happens to withdraw your invite as I'm certain that once we start down this road I will not be able to stop myself when the time comes and I will turn your life upside down.'

'Now you are worrying me.' I said unsure of what he was implying. 'It's only a drink; don't be so intense and get so wound up about it. You only need to stay for a little. Just show your face so to speak. It'll be good for you.'

'Yes you are right Francis. It will be good for me but knowing me will not be good for you I fear.'

'You're not a vampire or werewolf are you?' I said forcing a laugh in an attempt to make a joke of it. At that moment Lola walked in.

'Morning boys, are you both coming tomorrow after work then?' I nodded she looked at Geoff.

'Okay, but just for one drink.' His eyes held mine and I could not shake off the look he gave me for the rest of the day.

We were already at the Plume when Geoff arrived. I saw him at the door looking around nervously. I knew he was looking for me and not just our group. I was sure if he did not see me he would have gone. Suddenly I realised what the look had felt like that he had given me the previous day. It was that of a predator looking upon his prey. I felt as though I wanted to hide away so that he would not see me but just as I was about to turn he saw me and waved. I nodded back to him and took a large gulp from my pint.

'Hello Geoff, you made it then. I half expected not to see you after yesterday's conversation.'

'Oh that; don't worry about that. Can I buy you a drink?' he smiled I had never seen him smile. He looked different. I nodded 'go on then.' He came back with another pint for me and a large whisky for himself. I realised what was different. He looked neat and tidy. He had shaved and brushed his hair. He did not look so tired.

'You look much better today.' He nodded.

'Yes. I reached a turning point yesterday; with your help.' He looked at me with that predatory look that once again made me feel nervous. 'I have made a decision. I now know what I must do and I am not going to look back.'

'Good for you.' I replied

'I had a choice. End my life or take the steps I intend to take and not worry about the consequences.'

'That's a bit drastic isn't it?' I said not sure where this was leading. He nodded watching me intently. I took refuge in my beer, drinking deeply. I was saved by the arrival of Lola and Abigail.

'Hey looks like the drinks are on me then Francis.' I nodded forcing a smile. 'You're looking good Geoff. Nice to see you looking more relaxed than you usually do in the office.'

'Thank you; I've decided it's time to change.' Once again he directed his look at me.

'Help me get some drinks Francis.' said Lola, grabbing my arm. As we walked to the bar she whispered. 'What have you done to him? He's tidied himself up. He can't take his eyes off you. He's not gay is he?'

'I don't know; he's certainly different. He's been talking a bit weird though.' I paused, thinking about our conversations. 'Can't be gay though can he? You said yourself he's got a gorgeous wife.' They ordered the drinks and stood at the bar waiting. 'Anyway how do you know he's got a gorgeous wife?'

'Oh he had a problem with his car some time back. I was the only one in the office so dropped him home. She was at the door. He's got a huge house. God knows how he can afford that.' she turned and looked at me. 'I've been trying to work out what was strange about it though and I've just realised. It had two front doors.'

'That'll be £8.20 please madam,' said the bar man before I could comment. Lola dug into her purse.

'You need a mortgage just to buy a round of drinks.'

'Here I'll carry these across.' We soon joined our swelling group of work colleagues and general conversation buzzed around. I kept myself carefully away from Geoff, but kept getting the uncomfortable feeling that his eyes were upon me.

The following day I found myself in the office with only Lola to keep me company. At mid-morning she came across with a mug of tea for me.

'Here come and have a look at this.' She said in a hushed conspiratorial voice. Her eyes on the door to make sure no one was coming in, she lead me across to Geoff's desk. She pulled open the bottom draw and removed a picture in a frame which she passed to me. 'Found it when I was looking for a stapler,' she said sheepishly. The picture had been upside down in the draw. I turned it over. It was a picture of a beautiful blond woman standing in a doorway.

'That's his wife.'

'Wow, how'd he get someone like that?' I studied the girl in the picture. She was blonde and large-chested. She had a face like that of a doll; perfect smooth rounded cheeks and large blue eyes that seemed to look right into you even from the picture. She was quite small, but then I thought so is Geoff. She looked like she had just stepped out of a magazine photograph. She was not my type but she was certainly captivating. 'How do you know it's his wife?' I looked at Lola, who kept looking at the door to make sure no one was coming. She pointed to the house.

'It's the house I dropped him off at. Look you can see the two front doors.' I studied the background, finding it difficult as my eyes were constantly drawn to the woman. She stood in the left hand door, which was open behind her, but to her left there was another door. The frame was identical to the one she stood in but this one was closed.

'Oh yes... how strange.'

'Quick someone's coming.' Lola grabbed the photo from me and dropped it back into the draw. We both quickly returned to our desks before the door was open. I felt that my face had reddened with guilt at peeping into someone else's private life.

It was Geoff. He nodded to us both as he came in. We smiled back, guilt written all over our faces. Lola turned to me and pointed surreptitiously at the draw to Geoff's desk. To my horror I noticed that it was open. Lola had not had time to close it. I watched as Geoff sat down, looked at the drawer, picked out the photo and for a moment studied it. His brow creased into a deep frown. He looked up at us his pupils small and dark, then as quickly looked away. With a dramatic air he dropped the picture back into the drawer and closed it with a loud thud. I saw

Lola jump. I looked down at my work trying to hide my shame.

II

During the next month, as Christmas drew closer, Geoff seemed to burst from his shell. He was always dressing smartly, looking fresh and tidy. His dark hair slicked back, his brown eyes sparkling. As the rest of us seem to diminish and become paler in the cold short winter days, he seemed to be growing stronger and looking healthier. He chatted to everyone although I had noticed that, although he would constantly watch me and always said hello, he was not prepared to engage in conversation with me. I found that I felt rather relieved at this but could not fathom what was going on with him. Although I have to say most of the time I did not dwell on it, work was busy as was home as my family prepared for Christmas.

My children and I had put up the Christmas tree with the Christmas carol CD blaring away. Their long Christmas lists had been prepared and my wife was struggling through manic shoppers trying to get all that was needed. I loved this time, the anticipation in the children and the adults, the Christmas lights on in the evening, sitting with my wife curled up on the sofa in front of the fire watching the television, a gin and tonic in my hand. This year Christmas was going to be busy as both sets of our parents were coming over for Christmas day lunch. We all got on well as we had known each other for many years and family dramas were minimal.

Suffice to say Christmas went well and returning to work on the 27th December was a sad day but it was not long to the New Year break and snow was forecast. Tobogganing with the kids was always a winter highpoint. As I reluctantly walked into the office on that grey December morning I discovered that there were not too many of us in. Geoff was sitting at his desk as usual. He once again looked shabby and dishevelled. I guessed Christmas had not gone well and did not pry, although it was not long before he came over to me.

'Hi Francis, did you have a good Christmas?' Although I was dying to go into detail about the delights of my Christmas I could tell he was not really interested and had other things on his mind.

'Yes, it was good, the family were all together. I always enjoy those moments.' He looked at me and for an instant I thought he was going to cry.

'Yes me to.' He looked out of the window staring up at those low grey clouds, scudding over the roof tops. 'I missed them terribly.' I could not make sense of his reply.

'Were you not at home then?' He seemed confused his mind not on our conversation. 'You said you missed your family, I was wondering if you were not at home with them.'

'Oh I see, well yes I was but I wasn't.' Now it was my turn to look confused. 'You will understand. I can't really explain at present, but now I must, really must carry on with my plan, for better or worse. You will hopefully understand when your time comes.'

'Sorry Geoff. You're speaking in riddles mate. Either me or you have had too much to drink over the last few days.'

'Talking of drink; would you be available to pop in after work for a New Year's Eve drink at my place? My, err..; my wife is keen to meet you.' He could see I was not keen, 'Just one drink; only an hour.'

'I'll think about it Geoff if that's ok with you; not sure what we have planned. We usually go over to my parents – in – law.'

Geoff did not forget that he had asked me and continued to check to see whether I could go each morning. Each time I did not give him a definitive answer he looked more frantic until on the morning of the 31st he implored me to come.

'You have to come. Please!' There were tears in his eyes now. 'Please it's my wife you see...' I did not see and he did not explain. I had discussed it with my wife and she had not been keen as she wanted to get over to her parents as early as possible. In the end I had said that if I could not get out of it I would meet them there. At present I could not see a way out. I was beginning to think that if I said no he would break down and beg me to go.

'Okay' I agreed 'Just for an hour then I'll have to be off.'

So, on the 31st at the end of the day, we drove off towards his house, he led in his car and I followed behind. He did not live far from the office and we soon arrived at his quiet suburban street. All the houses were of a similar design bar one which stood out immediately. Geoff pulled up at this house. It was big, twice as big as the other detached houses in the street. A wide garden path led up to its two huge front doors surmounted by a large pointed arch, which I recognised from the photo. They looked out of place, too big for the house, as if they belonged to a church or temple. Christmas lights glistened from the eaves in the evening light. Two large bay windows either side of the doors, both had twinkling Christmas trees in them. I was impressed by the house's size; certainly way above our income capacity. I stopped on the road and got out. Geoff had pulled up on the large drive and jumped out quickly. He rushed across to me.

'Like the house,' I said. 'How the heck do you pay for all this?' He looked at me flustered.

'Oh there are no bills. It is the house I always wanted. It is part of the dream. At least I think it is; after the last few years I am no longer sure.'

'You're talking in riddles again.' I said not understanding what he was going on about.

'Sorry Francis, I cannot explain. You will understand soon.' He looked away unable to face me. I saw tears in his eyes. He guided me along the front path to the left hand door.

'Bit odd isn't it Geoff; two front doors.' I looked at him intrigued.

'It's a quirk of the house, nothing to do with me.' He mumbled not wanting to elaborate.

'I like the door knockers.' We had just reached the door. The huge door knocker on the left hand door, which had an identical twin on the right hand door, was a large bronzed head with two bearded faces looking in different directions. They looked old, ancient even. The bronze had turned green. 'They look like the figure of an ancient Greek god.'

'Another quirk of the house,' Geoff said, refusing to look at me. His voice sounded strained and anxious. He seemed keen to move on but did not seem to want to open the door. 'They are images of a god. Not Greek though – Roman. It is the god Janus.'

'Arr, don't know if I have heard of him.'

'He is associated with doors.' He stared at the door knocker his eyes transfixed, 'New beginnings, endings;' suddenly he fixed me with a penetrating stare; I shivered involuntarily; 'and duplicity,' He finished. I felt a sudden fear and a need to run but before I could even think of excuses to leave his eyes filled with tears and he covered his face. 'Oh that it has come to this. Now I have reached this point I don't know if I can continue.' He looked up at me his face now contorted in anguish. Unsure what to do I patted his arm and reached for the door handle saying,

'Come on let's get you in. I can see that a drink is definitely needed.' He raised his hand in what looked like a half-hearted attempt to stop me but I had already pushed the handle down and the door swung open, on two huge bronze hinges decorated with the figure of a woman, revealing a large hallway. I looked at him. He suddenly seemed resigned his shoulders sagged and he beckoned with his arm for me to enter. I stepped in and he followed. Once in the hallway he grabbed my arm, spinning me around.

'I am truly sorry,' he said. Once again I felt the need just to get out but was unsure how.

'Oh don't be silly.' I said as much to myself as him. 'What have you got to apologise for?' before he could answer a female voice behind me said.

'Hello, welcome.' I guessed it must be Geoff's wife so turned back to look into the hallway. She took me by surprise and I stumbled out a vague 'hello' in return. Before me was not the good looking blonde woman who I had taken for Geoff's wife but a veritable goddess. If I had to put together the perfect looking woman this would be her. She was a brunette, her hair long and hanging over her shoulders. Her face smooth unblemished, high cheekbones, bright blue eyes sparkling back at me. I could not stop my eyes as they scanned her body, my mind registering the perfect curves. I looked at Geoff, feeling swamped in confusion. I knew my cheeks were red from the long guilt ridden stare I had given the goddess before me.

'This is Carna.' Geoff said looking at me and refusing to look at the woman.

'Your wife?' Geoff nodded and mumbled

'At present I guess.' I turned and looked at her she stood waiting. She smiled and appeared unperturbed that Geoff seemed to be ignoring her.

'I thought she had blonde...'

'Ah, the photo, yes I thought you had looked at it.' He paused for a moment, weighing up what he intended to say. 'So she appears different.' I nodded looking at her. She continued to watch us not interfering. She just smiled every time I caught her eye. It was unnerving. 'She is what you most want to see. I see blonde you see...' I could not take my eyes off her now feeling totally transfixed.

'Brunette,' I stuttered.

'Welcome' she says again looking directly into my eyes 'I have been waiting for you Francis.' She stepped forward. Suddenly Geoff took my hand and placed it in hers. I feel slightly stunned; unable to react to what is happening, totally confused. She leant forward and kissed me on the lips. I feel their warm moisture. I am overwhelmed by the musky smell of her perfume. I looked at Geoff questioningly.

'I must go.' He said in a rush and quickly darts across to the right hand door. I watched him wanting to call him, follow him but feeling that my body is made of lead, my mind intoxicated by the woman who held my hand. He opened the door. Looking through it I saw bright sunshine. Quickly I looked through the door I had just entered and saw darkness. Through one shone the bright sun through the other the wane light of a full moon.

'Geoff!' I called. I tried at last to move but found I could not.

19

'Sorry Francis. You are a good man. It has to be this way. In time you will understand.' He looked sadly at me but I noticed his shoulders were now back, the anguish had gone and he smiled as he turned and looked out into the bright day of the right hand door. He gave me one last look then stepped quickly through the door and closed it behind him. The moment it shut it seemed to release me.

'What's going on?' I said almost shouting and looked at the woman before me. She reached up and kissed me again.

'Hello darling, welcome home.' I dropped her hand and pushed her back.

'What do you mean?' I felt dizzy. The hallway seemed to be changing around me as I looked at her. The stairway became more sweeping and the woodwork darker and more delicate. The carpeted floor slowly changed to black and white chequered tiles. 'My ideal hall' I thought with some dread. I ran across to the right hand door; the one Geoff had just exited by and pulled at the handle. It would not open. It was locked but there was no lock. I looked back at Carna. She just smiled back at me waiting. I went across to the other door, which was still open and went out, feeling the fresh cold December night air wash over me. I took a deep breath and looked around. Geoff was nowhere in sight. His car had gone. Strangely mine was now parked on the drive instead. I know that I had left it locked on the road. I checked my pockets for the keys, pulling them out; car key and house key were both still there. My head was spinning in confusion. I looked back into the house. She still stood there watching me. 'What trick is this?!' I shouted at her.

'There's no trick my darling.' She said calmly walking to the door. 'This is how it is.'

'And what is that supposed to mean then.' I shouted back at her angrily. I felt the adrenalin buzzing through my veins as I tried to deal with this surreal situation. I felt the edges of my vision blur and change as I watched her. For a moment I dreaded looking for fear of what I would see. Eventually gaining the courage I looked at the house. It was changing, just as the hallway had done. An elegant modern Georgian style house was slowly appearing. 'My dream house,' I thought, closing my eyes. 'I must be dreaming, count to ten, take a deep breath, it will all be gone then.' With my eyes closed I slowly counted. '…8, 9, 10,' slowly I opened my eyes. Carna was still watching me from the doorway, waiting. My dream Georgian style house stood before me. I shook my head unable to accept it.

'I must go.' I muttered, and turned, stumbling to my car.

'Drive carefully,' Carna called. 'See you soon.'

'Not if I can help it,' I thought. Though, I could not get her picture out of my head. It was as if she had been created from my mind. Beauty in a woman as I would perceive it, a too perfect, perfection; she could not be real. I shook my head, trying to convince myself that soon I would wake up and backed the car off the drive. I saw her waving as I drove away.

My heart rate slowed and I began to feel that things had returned to normal as I drove across the town; back to my family, my home, my reality. I wondered if all that I perceived had just happened, was real. It had felt so real. I remembered it all clearly. I was sure it must be a dream, but did that mean I was still dreaming. After all I had not woken up to find myself in my comfortable bed with my wife deep in sleep beside me.

I wondered if I had nodded off and it had all happened in a sort of suspended dream time, a flash dream. If this was the case it was lucky I had not crashed. Although I remembered occasions when I had driven home at the end of a busy day but not remembered the journey; Just sort of getting home on auto pilot. After all I felt it was very hard to judge with dreams whether the time of the sleep equals the time of the dream.

I had read somewhere of a seventeenth century philosopher, who said that we cannot trust what our senses tell us, that dreams and reality could feel one and the same. So I thought 'was I dreaming or was it all real.' This philosopher was known as a rationalist and believed in the importance of reason in determining reality. My rationalism told me it could not be real. It did not fit my pattern of what is real. Houses do not just change in front of you, except at the movies. I came to the conclusion I must have been dreaming and with a sigh, concentrated on my driving although I could not quite rid myself of the vision of the beautiful Carna.

III

Finally I turned into my estate and wound my way through the confusing maze of streets and very similar small modern houses. Turning onto my street, I jammed the breaks on, coming to an emergency stop, the wheels skidding on bitumen. The street was much as it always was the small detached houses set back slightly from the road, lit by the neon glow of the street lamps. The houses in this street were all of the same design, four small bedrooms, and garage to the side.

But now where my small house had stood there seemed to be a larger plot, much larger, as if the physicality of that small plot had been stretched beyond the normal dimensions of this world. I realised I had seen something similar once before but not really noticed at the time and that was at Geoff's. My house no longer stood on that plot; it had been replaced by a large modern red brick Georgian style house with a long drive leading up to a double garage. It was the house I had just left.

I just sat stunned, in my car, in the road until I was disturbed by a car honking me as it manoeuvred around me.

'This can't be,' I mumbled to myself. I pulled over and got out. There was a dusting of snow coming down. The air was cold, my breath visible. All these things I could feel. The rest of the street was exactly as I remembered it when I had driven out that morning shouting at the children to get downstairs, be good and get ready, then giving my wife a quick kiss at the doorstep of our house; a house that was now no longer there. I held my hand out and caught a snow flake. Its perfect crystalline shape slowly melted in my palm. It was all too real.

Walking slowly, my footsteps muffled by the snow, I approached the large impostor of a house. I stood before it on the pavement. It was exactly how I would want it to look except it had two huge front doors; out of place on this house, so big they reached up into the second floor. On those doors I noticed huge bronze door knockers depicting the god that I knew was called Janus and those large eye catching hinges. Studying them more closely I realised that the woman depicted on them was naked and stylised as a goddess. I began to walk up the long path, thinking, 'who cares if the house has changed as long as my wife and children are inside' but a deep foreboding filled me with dread as I reached the large left hand door. I was about to try it but thought better of it and went across to the right hand door. I tried this one but it was locked. I was not surprised to see that there was no key hole, no lock. Walking back to the other door I pushed down on the handle. To my surprise it too was locked. This one did have a key hole in a large old fashioned bronze lock. Suddenly I felt a slight weight in my pocket. With a trembling hand I reached in, knowing that the key I should have was modern and small and would never open this door. I pulled out my key ring with car key and house key but instead of my little modern key, a large gold key hung in its place. Before I put the door key in I knew it was going to fit. It slipped in perfectly and turning it the door swung open.

I did not want to step in, onto that chequered hall way. I was not ready to face the person who I knew would be in there. I pulled the door closed and went back to my car. It was a while before I could conjure up any thought of what to do. Eventually I pulled out my phone. I would ring Rosie, my wife. I touched the screen to show my contacts and scrolled down to Rosie, but her name was no longer there. I searched for my son and daughters phone numbers, my parents-in-law they were no longer there. Finally with a fatal inevitability I scrolled back to C and there she was – CARNA.

'No it was not possible' my reason would not let me believe that this was real. I started the car and drove off. The roads were quiet. The snow fell slowly down. After an hour of meandering around the town I returned. The Georgian house still stood there. I decided I needed to see people; normal people to reinforce reality then when I came back my house would be there with my family. I drove to my local, the Coach and Horses.

When I opened the door the heat and the cacophony of voices washed over me. The smell of sweat, aftershave, perfume and above all alcohol invaded my nostrils. 'This has to be real' I thought. Walking in, I pushed my way through the mass of New Year's Eve revellers until I reached the bar.

'Hello there Francis' said the barman 'thought I'd see you in here at some point. Do you want your usual?'

'Err...' I was caught out for a moment. I came in here every now and then but I did not have a 'usual' and I did not really know the barman.

'Move out of the way Paul,' said a Barmaid, pushing the man behind the bar and squeezing round behind him. 'Oh hello Francis how's that lovely wife of yours? You haven't brought her with you tonight?'

'He never does,' said Paul the barman, 'more's the pity.'

'You shouldn't perv after other men's wives,' said the barmaid laughing and hitting him on the arm.

'Why not, Francis doesn't mind, do you? And she is a corker that one.' My thoughts once again began to spin out of control. The only times I ever came to the pub was with Rosie and we sat quietly in the corner. 'Are you on your usual tonight then Francis?'

'Err. Yes.' I stuttered back. I watch as he took a tumbler and measured out two shots of Scottish single malt. Almost in a panic I thought 'I don't drink whisky!' Surely this dream which I was now classing as a nightmare would end soon. And yet it felt more real than any dream I had ever had. It felt the way reality should.

I took the drink and paid the barman. Taking a careful sip I found myself enjoying the warm sensation of the liquid flowing down into my stomach, the raw peat flavour invading my senses. The memory of past encounters with this particular drink was that of harsh raw bitterness that sent a shiver down my spine. I leant against the bar watching the animated crowd enjoying the last hours of the year. 'What do I do now?' I wondered as my body slowly warmed and my mind calmed down. I pulled out my phone to check again that the numbers for my family were no longer there; that Carna's number was there.

'Hello there, Francis!' It was a shout from across the room. I looked up and saw my next door neighbour waving at me to come over and join him. I hesitated, fearing the contact, fearing what he was going to say. He was insistent with his waving so I weaved my way through the throng.

'Hello Peter' I said warily. I saw his wife perched on a chair around a table chatting to a group of women. She waved and smiled

'Carna not with you, Francis?' I shook my head, and felt my shoulders sag. For a moment I thought that she was going to ask me about Rosie who she had got on so well with. I shook my head.

'Been at work today have you?' said Peter looking me up and down. 'Look as though you need more time off. Are you okay?'

'Yes, I guess so; as good as can be expected anyway.' I replied.

'You been off at all in the Christmas period?'

'Had a few days over Christmas. I've got tomorrow off as well.'

'Glad I've seen you' he said, 'Because I wanted to chat to you about the hedge.'

'Hedge?' I replied my assaulted brain struggling. I saw Peter's wife look up at Peter with a disapproving look; a, not here, not now look.

'Yes the hawthorn hedge at the front that borders our properties.'

'Hawthorn hedge' I mumbled. I did not have a hawthorn hedge at least I did not in my old memory.

'That house of yours is so big you don't even notice, ha,' said Peter laughing at my confusion. 'Mind the hawthorn goes right round your property doesn't it?' not sure how to reply I nodded a vague assent. 'It's just that it's getting a bit high don't you think. It's started to block the sun out from our front windows. Wondered if it was possible to trim it back?' he saw my uncertainty as did his wife and they mistook it for a negative answer.

'We could do it' she said 'at the front there anyway.'

'Err yes, can't see a problem with that.' I saw the relief on their faces. I drank back the last of my whisky. Waited for its warmth to hit my stomach then said I needed to get going and made an exit for the door.

I could not seem to escape this and wondered if I was going insane yet just a few hours ago everything had been so normal. I sat back in the car and wondered what to do. Did I go to the house that now appeared to be home and to the woman who now seemed to be my wife? What else could I do? I could contact my parents but they would find that strange as they had gone to my brothers for the New Year. They usually rang us after midnight to wish us a happy new year.

I decided to visit my parents-in-law; that is Rosie's parents, who did not live far away and who we were meant to be visiting to welcome in the New Year. I set off, pleased that I had some sort of a plan. The drive to their house took an hour as the snow was now falling quite hard. It was coming up for nine o'clock.

I pulled into their drive. At least that felt familiar. This was definitely their house. I got out, feeling strangely nervous. Ringing the door bell, I waited, feeling the snow slowly cover my head and shoulders. I rang again my nervousness making me impatient. Eventually the door was answered.

'Oh hello, sorry I thought you were a group of boys that keep coming round pretending to be carol singers. Can't sing a note they can't. Don't even know any carols past the first line. Mind they know how to be abusive if you don't give them anything. What can I do for you?'

'Hello Matilda.' She looked at me slightly confused and with a sinking feeling I knew she did not recognise me. A man came up behind her looking concerned. I recognised Harry, Rosie's father. They looked at each other bemused, trying to place me. 'I'm a friend of Rosie's.' I tried, thinking that saying 'husband' could cause greater confusion.

'Rosie?' I saw a tear form in the corner of Matilda's eye.

'I'm sorry sir, I think you must have the wrong place,' said Harry, putting his arm around his wife protectively.

'Harry?' he looked sharply at me.

'How do you know us?' I could see a fear in his eyes. His hand gripped Matilda's shoulder tighter.

'You have a daughter called Rosie?' I persisted.

'We did, she died when she was just a child, an accident,' said Matilda, with more tears developing.

'What do you want from us? We don't know you,' said Harry getting angry. 'It's New Year's eve for God's sake!' Matilda looked worried now.

'I'm sorry I didn't want to upset you. It's just...' I looked at Harry's face and knew I would get no further. 'Sorry.' I finished lamely and went back to my car. I backed out of their drive not daring to look at them. I could feel their eyes following me as I drove away. It was late now and the snow on the road was building up. I knew I had no choice now I had to just drive back to ... Do I call it home, not yet anyway, but the place where home should be. Carefully, with wheels spinning I headed back. The roads were so bad that they took all my concentration. I was unable to ponder on what would be waiting for me.

It was coming up to eleven o'clock when I reached my street. Driving carefully down the unsalted road I pulled onto the drive of the large Georgian style house that appeared to be my home. This time I noticed the huge hawthorn hedge topped with a covering of snow that appeared to surround the property. I walked up to the large front doors and with shaking hand pushed the gold key once again into the lock of the left hand one. It swung open smoothly and with resignation I stepped onto the chequered tiled floor of the hallway. Swinging the door closed behind me I shook off the snow and watched it fall to the floor and melt. I looked back at the two doors closed behind me. Between them stood a large vase, roman in style filled with what looked like sprigs of Hawthorn, covered in flowers.

Hearing a sound I looked up. Carna had stepped through a door leading off from the hall to my left and stood watching me. The look of her took my breath away. She seemed to overwhelm my senses. I shook my head trying to clear my fuddled thoughts.

'Hello darling, you're back.' She stated. She approached me, I felt unable to move. She kissed me on the lips, long and lingering. The smell of her filled my nostrils. I felt dizzy. I managed to lift my arms and pull her away, holding her at arm's length.

'What is happening?' she reached up and took my hand, smiling, she lead me through the door through which she had entered into a large comfortable lounge. She pulled my damp jacket from my shoulders and threw it onto a sofa.

'Let me get you a drink.' she said walking to a sideboard with bottles and glasses on it. I studied the room. A fire roared in a large fire place filling the room with comfortable warmth. Oil paintings hung on the walls, countryside scenes and seascapes. Framed photos and ornaments sat on an elegant sideboard. Looking closer I noticed that they were photos of Carna and myself. I looked quickly away from them. A large Christmas tree filled one corner of the room. Christmas cards seemed to fill every spare available space. Deep comfortable sofas sat each side of the fire with a coffee table between them. I was surprised to notice that there was no television. 'Here' Carna handed me a cut crystal tumbler. 'Your favourite, Islay single malt,' I held the glass up. The fire light flickered in the amber liquid. I took a large gulp, feeling the peaty fire burn down my throat. The smell of it flared my nostrils and shook me out of my reverie.

'You haven't answered my question.'

'Sit,' she said pointing to one of the sofas. I sat. She sat down opposite me curling her legs up onto the sofa. 'What will be, will be.'

'What's that supposed to mean?'

'This is your life. It is up to you how you live' she looked sadly at me. I noticed that for all her perfection she looked tired.

'Am I dreaming?'

'What is dreaming? Where does dreaming end and reality start.'

'Is this real then?'

'She reached over and grabbed my hand. You can feel it. What do your senses tell you?'

'Can I trust them?' she just smiled sadly.

'That is for you to decide.'

'It does not feel right.'

'Many things in life do not feel right but in the end we get used to them and finally do not realise that they ever felt wrong.'

'I have memories of another life only a few hours old.' I gulped down the last of the whisky enjoying the flavour as it swirled around my mouth and down my throat. It felt so real and yet I did not like whisky! There were so many contradictions.

The single malt began to pulse through my veins. I felt anger growing. I wanted to hit her, shake her, throw things, smash the house up looking for a way out. I threw the tumbler into the fire. It shattered, scattering crystals of glass amongst the burning logs. A few drops of whisky hissed and burst into flame disappearing just as quickly. The shards of glass crackled and cracked in the heat.

My anger dispersed as quickly as it had come. I was not one to lose my temper and I was surprised by my actions. I looked across at her feeling my face burn with shame and guilt.

'I still don't understand...' I paused, 'comprehend what is happening.' I looked into her deep blue eyes, the colour of a bottomless sea. They sucked me in, calmed me but held no answer.

The elegant antique French clock on the mantel piece began to chime. Carna reached down and filled two glasses from a bottle on the table and handed one to me. I saw that the bottle label read Moet and Chandon.

'Happy New Year.' The words seemed to caress me as if they were an echo which continued to float through endless time. I drank down the champagne feeling the alcohol slowly flooding the synapses in my head and enjoying the numbing affect it was creating. Reaching across I grabbed the bottle and refilled my glass. The more I had the better, I thought. The phone in the hall began to ring. I looked uncertainly at Carna.

'It's for you, you go.' I moved hesitantly across the room and out into the hall. An old fashioned telephone stood on a stand. I had not noticed it before. I picked up the receiver and mumbled, 'Hello'

'Francis darling, Happy New Year.'

'Mother?'

'Yes of course, Happy New Year. Your dad's here too.' I heard her goading him to speak.

32

'Happy New Year son,' He called.

'And to you, too.' I replied my heart racing; now I could get this sorted out, surely.

'Have you two had a good evening?'

'Two?' now I began to feel nervous.

'Yes dear, you've had too much to drink haven't you?' She did not wait for an answer. 'I mean you and that beautiful wife of yours, Carna.'

'Hmm.' I did not know what to say. My mouth was dry and I began to cough and splutter.

'Put her on dear, as I can see as usual you haven't got much to say. Just like your father. At least I'll find out how you both are if I have a chat to her.' I put the phone on the table and turned but Carna was there beside me. She picked up the receiver and began to chat happily to my mother. My mother! The thought crashed through my head. I staggered back into the lounge and collapsed onto the sofa, cradling my head in my hands as I listened to the laughter and chatter in the hallway. I looked up as it suddenly went quiet and I heard the receiver being replaced. Carna put her head round the door.

'I am going to bed now, I think.' I returned her gaze uncertainly.

'Is that an invitation?'

'Do you need one? This is your house. I am your wife. I am always there for you.' She smiled. Before I could answer she turned and headed out of the door. I heard her walk up the stairs.

I sat back, there was no way that I was ready for sleep; plus going upstairs with her would give me a bedroom dilemma that I was not ready to face. I sank into the deep comfortable sofa and watched the fire crackling, the flames jumping and flicking in mesmerising patterns.

My thoughts were becoming befuddled by the alcohol. I felt exhausted by the emotional rollercoaster that did not seem to want to stop. I wondered if I slept that I would wake up in my own bed at home. I thought of Rosie and wondered where she was; what she was doing; what my children were doing. Did they actually exist? That thought frightened me. I pulled out my wallet, remembering that I had a picture of us all together from our last holiday on the Corsican coast. My hands shaking slightly I opened my wallet. There was a picture of Carna and myself standing on a beach with a blue Mediterranean sea behind us. I shook my head I just could not believe it. I was not prepared to let go. My mind wrestling with the strangeness of my situation I continued to drink the champagne until tipping the bottle up I found it empty.

I stood up a little unsteadily and decided to look around. After all I thought, chuckling to myself, this is my house and I do not even know what it looks like. Then I thought, well, if this is a product of my imagination perhaps if I imagine what it is like it will be so. I tried to picture what my dream house would look like.

'Library with lots of books, a wood panelled study. TV games room. Modern kitchen with some old fashioned style, a large farmhouse table and Aga and a dining room ' I thought to myself ' oh yes and a swimming pool and gym, if it is from my imagination lets have as much as possible.' with this in mind I set off to explore.

There was a door in the corner of the room which I had not seen before. I had the unnerving feeling it had not been there. I went over and walked through into a large library full of old books; a polished round table sat in the middle of the room with papers on it. I turned and walked through another door that led into my wood panelled study. My legs were shaking slightly. These rooms had just come from my imagination. I knew that if I continued to look I would find the others just as I had thought of them earlier. Leaving the study I crossed the hall into a large kitchen, a large pine farmhouse table at its centre. I continued through the kitchen into the dining room; from the high ceiling, hung a chandelier over a long dark polished dining table. Shaking my head now I walked through into the hallway coming out by the front doors.

I remembered Geoff's words about the doors 'nothing to do with me. They came with the house.' So this was something more than just a dream, just my imagination. Walking along the hall past the stairs and the door ways to the kitchen on the right and the study on the left I came to the back of the house. Opening the door I could see a building in the garden; its lights on, reflecting in the water of the swimming pool beneath them and glistening across the snow covered lawn.

I wandered back to the lounge deep in thought. The mantel piece clock now striking one am. So the house or most of it was my imagination, the girl, or at least the way she looked was too. Yet the doors of the house were not and I never would have thought of a name like Carna. Besides in my imagination I would share my perfect house with my perfect family and they seem to have disappeared, wiped away without a trace apart from the memories that I held of them. I felt tears stream down my cheeks as my emotions finally got the better of me. I missed them I needed them, without them this was all worthless. I lay curled up on the sofa the sobs coming thick and fast, my body shaking with emotional pain. I prayed for sleep to take me away and return me to my normality when I woke.

IV

A clock was chiming somewhere close, I woke, aching and uncomfortable, my mouth clammy, and my head thumping from alcohol. I knew before I opened my eyes that I was not in my bed. That even after sleep I was in the House, the Janus House. The two faces of the god from the front doors seemed to be burning through my eyelids, watching me, severe and unswerving. The only sound now was the quiet tick of the clock. I opened my eyes, sat up and looked across at the mantel piece. The old ornate clock struck six am. The embers of the fire beneath it glowed up at me, warm and comforting, except that was not how I felt and they could not overcome the cold emptiness that seemed to fill me.

I got up and searched out a bathroom beneath the stairs then went into the kitchen and made some coffee. Somehow things seemed to be in the drawers I expected them to be in.

So what to do, It was New Year's Day. As I drank my coffee in the quiet of the morning I made a resolution. I would not forget or give up my quest for answers but I had to accept and live as best as I could and see where this journey would take me for I was certain there must be a way back.

The moment I had come to this decision I heard a sound behind me. It was as if she had known. She stood in a shear thin negligee that hugged her body. Even in the state I was in, I felt an overwhelming sense of desire. She put her arm on me. I wondered how I would be able to deal with this, to stay true to the image of my wife, I just did not know.

'Good morning, any coffee left?' she yawned and tousled her hair, her every move cut at my efforts to hold on to the resolution I had only just made.

'Yes, in the pot there. Fill me up please.' She took my cup poured the coffees and sat down opposite me. I tried not to look at her breasts visible through the thin material.

'I'm not...'

'I understand. You need time. Use the spare room.' I nodded at her.

'That makes sense.'

'I am there for you when you are ready.'

'I thought when I woke up...' I drank some coffee and looked up at her. 'Can you explain what is happening?' she shook her head but I could see in her eyes that she knew. 'Do I still like fishing?'

'Of course you do. Your equipment is in your study.' I nodded. Not knowing what else to do. I thought it might be a good idea, get me away from the House. It was something I always did when I needed to get away on my own to sort out problems.

'Perhaps I'll go out fishing today; Time to think. You know.' She smiled. It melted into me. This was going to be hard.

'Yes that would be good for you.' She got up. 'I must get dressed. Then I'll make you some breakfast and get you a flask to take with you. Go and have a swim. It will freshen you up and relax you.'

A covered walkway led through the melting snow to a small indoor heated pool. I stripped and jumped in allowing the water to flood over my body. Then after a short swim I climbed out. Returning to the house I grabbed some toast and yet another coffee and headed into the study. I had not noticed it the previous night but there next to the table stood the expensive rod that I had always wanted and in a box on the table the best sparkling silver reel I had ever seen. Once again it was the out of reach dream that I had seen in a fishing magazine. I grunted not wanting to dwell on it all just yet and packed up my gear. In the corridor I met Carna who appeared from the kitchen with a shoulder bag containing some food and a flask.

'Thank you.' Again I saw that sad smile in her eyes.

'Go enjoy, think. Come back.' I just nodded in reply and headed for the door.

I was soon trudging across the melting snow down to the local reservoir where I had always fished. The sky was clear, the morning bright. The world was quiet so early on New Year's Day. I was soon down on the shore setting up my rod and attaching the flies. I am a fly fisherman, trout is my game. The past year had not been very successful so I was expecting plenty of time to contemplate my present situation, especially as the sky was so bright and the water cold. The fish would not be moving. For once I was not here just to fish and enjoy the scenery. I was here to think and to escape.

Taking a deep breath of the cool fresh air, I cast out and slowly began to pull the line in. The cold of the water I was standing in started to creep through my wellingtons. To my surprise I got a bite. Excitement took over as I began the battle to haul in the fish. Suddenly it launched itself out of the water. A large Rainbow trout, I lost myself in the tug of war as the fish fought for its life. Eventually it was within reach and I waded out with the net, pulling in the beautiful fish, iridescent in the morning light. My heart racing, I pulled it ashore, and for the first time since leaving work the previous day, I forgot about my dilemma.

The fish was soon bagged and I cast out again. It was not long before I was hauling in another and then a third.

Within two hours I had bagged five and was beginning to wonder whether other powers were at work here. That was more than I had caught all year in a day's fishing. Was my imagination giving me success as it had given me the wonderful rod and reel? I paused for reflection. I could not deny that I had enjoyed the last couple of hours immensely. Sitting down I pulled out the flask and wondered if it was not my imagination was it Carna. Who was in control of what was going on with me? I sipped the warm tea in the morning light and looked around me. I could not be in a more beautiful place. The ripples in the water glistened like pearls. The trees dripped constantly with the melting snow that still coated the land.

As I watched a roe deer crept cautiously out of the trees and hesitantly made its way down to the water. It obviously was not used to company at this time in the morning. Reaching the water's edge it drank. I dare not move. It moved back along the shore line looking for exposed patches of winter grass. Suddenly it stopped and looked up. Our eyes met for the briefest moment then it was off bounding through the snow and back into the trees.

Its disappearance made me feel suddenly alone in the world. I shivered. The cold white land felt inhospitable. I shook my head; I needed a plan. After a moment's thought I decided that the best thing to do would be to go back to Geoff's house and confront him.

But before I left I could not resist a few more casts. Whether it was my imagination or Carna or Janus for that matter I was enjoying my success.

Over the next two hours unable to stop I landed another three fish. My best haul of the year and all in just four and a half hours. It was coming up to midday so I decided to head back to the house unload my fish have a bite to eat and then head out in search of Geoff.

Packing up my gear I trudged back to the House. My pace getting slower as the adrenalin from my success wore off and I got closer to 'home'. The snow had melted away from the roads and was dripping heavily from the trees and buildings as I walked through the estate to the House. People were now out and about. Some walking slightly aimlessly, recovering from the excesses of the previous night and unsure how to use the free time of the first day of the year, others were striding out with dogs. A few cars sloshed past. A family walked by me full of themselves and the excitement of the snow and their togetherness. I felt the pain of longing course through me.

Finding myself in front of the House I was once again confronted by the giant doors with the large bronze Janus doorknockers. They were daunting and I felt that they seemed to exude some sort of power. The air seemed to crackle as I moved in close to them. I wondered if they were the key to my change in circumstance. They were certainly the only thing unchanged from Geoff's house. I felt a shudder run through me as I pushed open the left hand door and walked in.

She greeted me at the door.

'Ah good you are back for lunch. Did you have any success?'

'You know I did.' I replied sharply. She looked at me hurt and I felt guilty. 'Sorry.' I apologised quickly. 'You did know I would though.' I continued unable to let it go. She smiled at me but did not reply.

'Come and eat with me.' I held up the heavy bag of fish. 'Put them in the utility.' She indicated with a nod of her head. 'We can sort them afterwards.' I followed the direction she had intimated through the back door and found myself in a large utility room where I placed them in the sink. When I had walked out of the house for my swim earlier I had not walked through this room. Stripping off my outdoor gear I went into the kitchen. Hot soup and chunky bread was waiting for me plus a glass of red wine. I gulped it down quickly as I sat down opposite Carna.

For a while we ate in silence. I actually felt strangely comfortable. I realised it was part of her persona. The only difficulty was sitting opposite the perfect product of your imagination and trying not to constantly stare at her. She certainly made it very difficult for me to focus on the predicament that I thought I was in. Eventually I broke the silence.

'You know what is happening don't you.' I studied her. She said nothing but the answer was written in her face. 'Tell me.' I was almost pleading.

'I cannot.'

'Why not? I don't understand.'

'I just cannot.'

'Why? Are you unable to?' I had a thought 'or are you not allowed to? Is it against the rules?' I had some idea that if this were coming from my imagination then my imagination would not allow her to give the game away. She nodded at me.

'Please, you must let it go then we can be happy together.' I shook my head.

'No, when I understand. Then maybe...' I smiled at her. 'I need to understand. 'If I am the one that's stopping you speaking; you know my imagination.' I did not quite know how to explain. 'Well let's just say I want you to speak to tell me I give you permission.'

'It's not you.' She looked away, gazing into the distance out of the kitchen window.

'Not me.' I echoed her. She shook her head. 'Not me.' I repeated thinking hard. She continued to look out at the melting snow. 'If it's not me, is it something else, someone else?' She turned suddenly and looked at me surprised.

'You are moving quickly.'

'Quicker than the others?' I do not know what made me say it but I had a vision of Geoff in a similar place in the past. Perhaps there were others before him. She nodded. 'So there were others?' she did not reply but I knew I was correct. My heart quickened. I felt at last I was getting somewhere.

'So something is stopping you and it's not me, my imagination.' I was talking to her but also to myself, trying to figure it all out. She did not speak, just watched me. 'Is it some sort of quiz or challenge?' Still she said nothing, careful to keep her face expressionless. I stood up and paced the kitchen. I could not seem to get any further. 'I need to go out for a drive, to think, you know.' She looked at me concerned. 'Don't worry I will come back. After all where else can I go? This seems to be my home.' She smiled at me and stood up.

'I will be waiting.' A sudden thought came to me as I looked into her perfect face.

'Will you ever be able to tell me?' She seemed to take pity on me.

'You must know when to ask me,' she replied. 'It is all I can say on it at present. Now what are your plans for this afternoon?' I could tell that she did not want me to go out again but said guiltily.

'I am just going out for a drive. I won't be long.'

42

'Where to?' I watched her face carefully as I replied.

'To see if Geoff is in. I fancy he owes me an explanation if you will not.' She flinched slightly and shook her head. 'I will see you later.' Grabbing my keys and jacket I left.

The snow was all but gone; a wet drabness was left behind. After the brilliant brightness of the morning whiteness everything now looked dark and grey; the trees just black skeletons that lined the road as I drove. I soon found that I needed the lights on. It did not take long to reach Geoff's house where only the day before I had visited, but this time the large house and grounds that had stood on the site were missing and was replaced by a normal estate house of the same mould as those around it. It was as though the street had contracted and squeezed it out; Just as my street had seemed to have expanded to fit in the huge house that I now seemed to own.

I walked pensively up to the door and rang the bell. A tired looking middle aged woman answered, with a couple of young children round her legs.

'Err… Good afternoon and err… Happy New Year.' I said.

'Happy New Year to you too. How may I help you?'

'Is Geoff in?' As soon as I finished a foreboding came over me.

'Sorry, Geoff? Do you want my husband? His name is not Geoff its Simon.'

'Simon' I mumbled, I should have known

'Si!' she called. A balding man came through a door carrying a newspaper.

'Ah hello; Can I help you?' he said studying me intently. He was not Geoff.

'Sorry I was looking for a Geoff.' I said 'I thought he lived here. I must have the wrong house.' The couple looked at each other.

'Can't think of a Geoff around here. Can you love?' she shook her head becoming distracted by the children. 'What's the surname?' I realised with a shock that I did not know. The man smiled at my confusion. 'Sorry, don't think I can help you.'

'Thanks anyway.' I said making my way to the car. I was just getting in when the front door of the house reopened behind me and the man poked his head out.

'Don't know if it helps.' He called 'but my wife just reminded me. The person we bought the house from last January was called Geoff. A Geoff Price it was. He had a wife and child.' I had stopped in my tracks. I knew this must be Geoff.

'Last January you say.' I walked back up the path. He nodded. 'You don't know where they went do you.' He turned and called into the house.

'Did they leave an address love?' his wife shouted back a no. 'Sorry again. Do you think it's who you are looking for?'

'Could be; thank you for the information.'

I was in deep thought as I drove back. I wondered whether it could be the same Geoff who had left a full year ago. How could that be? Unless... I remembered that when I had last seen him he had stepped through the right door, through which I had seen daylight and yet it had been dark through the door we had entered. Had he gone to a different time or perhaps a parallel universe? I felt that anything was possible now and wondered whether I would actually find him. I would have to wait for the following day to see if he showed at work.

Arriving back at the house I found Carna with her feet curled up in front of the fire reading a book. I went over to drinks cabinet and picked up the bottle of whisky. Carna's words from the previous night echoing in my head, 'Islay, your favourite.' I must have mumbled something as she watched me and said.

'Yes, it's an island in Scotland, in the inner Hebrides I believe. They have quite a few distilleries there.' I nodded and poured out a glass.

'Do you want a drink of anything? I'm afraid I don't know your favourite.' I said with a hint of sarcasm. I was still finding it difficult not to be angry at her.

'A glass of that Italian wine, please.' Pouring her a drink I went and sat opposite her.

'He wasn't there.' I said giving her the drink. The fire crackled in the hearth its warmth hitting the side of my face.

'No' was all she replied.

'You knew?' she nodded which did not surprise me. 'You could have saved me the journey.' I said with some resignation.

'No, it is your journey.'

'And what does that mean?'

'Look why don't you relax, let's talk of something different.'

'How can I? You are so frustrating, saying things but not explaining.' I sat back and studied her beauty as she returned to reading her book. Her long dark hair flowed down over her shoulders. Her skin had the look of the Mediterranean. Her face was defined not only by those sparkling eyes but by her high cheek bones. Her nose was delicate, not to proud not to slim. I knew I could not see a fault in her appearance because I was sure she had come from my imagination, but her personality, her thoughts they were something different. She appeared timeless and I wondered at her age.

'What are you reading?' I enquired. She lifted up her face and focused on me with a smile.

'Ovid'

'Sounds like an ancient classic.' I said wondering if even this was a clue.

'Yes he lived from 43 BC to 18 AD'

'So pretty old then! So that's the name of the author not title of the book.' She nodded; I could see that she was enjoying the conversation.

'Yes, he was a roman poet. His real name is Publius Ovidius Naso. I have the collection of his works.' She pointed to a book case in the corner of the room.

'The books look old'

'Yes, very.' There was a look of tenderness in her eyes. I could see this was a treasured possession, a definite window into her past and her mind I thought. She held it out for me to take and look at.

'Latin?' I said questioningly looking at the page that the book was open before me. The page was yellowed and ancient. The script was hand written. I wondered if this was produced pre the printing press, which would make it at least five hundred years old. It certainly looked it.

'Yes' she replied I could see she was keen to have the book back, her eyes never leaving it.

'So, you are fluent in Latin.' She nodded assent. I discovered I had finished my whisky and went over to refill. I realised I had a need for alcohol at present. It was helping me to cope with the massive changes in my life and to deal with my ever changing situation.

Sitting back down I asked her what the book was about. She explained that Ovid had written three volumes of erotic poetry the Heroides, Amores and Ars Amatoria, and he was also well known for his work called the Metamorphoses, a book called the Fasti, plus some poetry collections called Tristia and Epistulae ex Panto. I said I was going to have to find some English versions if hers were all in the original Latin.

'So is this guy your favourite author.'

'I guess so.'

'What about Homer and his Iliad, if you like the old stuff?'

'Good, but Greek. Ovid's a Roman.' That certainly got me thinking even with the warm fuzz of the fire and the whisky.

'So what is special about Rome? What's the connection?' She did not want to reply and got up to fill her glass.

'I was talking about authors' she muttered as she poured herself some more wine. She carried the glass out to the kitchen saying she had to prepare some food. I had not realised how late it had become it was dark outside. I should have felt comfortable sitting by the large roaring fire with my whisky in hand but I was restless and was soon standing up wandering the room. Walking into the study I sat down at the desk. The desk was clear so I began to look through the drawers.

In the top drawer I found a small leather note pad and some pens. I decided to write down what I knew and see if I could draw some conclusions or at least formulate some kind of plan as to what to do next. Opening the book I began to write.

1.   *As I have not returned to my previous existence I must assume that I am in some sort of reality. A place that I must at least come to terms with and perhaps live in forever. If I can!*

2.   *Everything had changed when I arrived with Geoff at his house. Note-need to find Geoff.*

3.   *What does Janus have to do with all this? Note -research Janus.*

4.   *Who is Carna? Why did she appear different to me? Why will she not tell me what has happened? I am sure she knows. Why did she say you must know when to ask me?*

5.   *The House. Why two front doors?*

6.   *What happened to my family? Why did Rosie's parents say she had died when she was young?*

7.   *Above all hold onto the memory of Rosie, my wife and my children Theresa and Michael*

I was about to stop when I remembered our recent conversation and added

8.   *What is special about Ovid or his books?*

9.   *Is Rome, Latin important? It seems to be to Carna.*

I looked at my list wondering if I had missed anything then decided I could add more as I go.

I looked in the other drawers of the desk and found a laptop. Pulling it out, I wondered if I would be able to access and decided that I must be able to as it was my study and desk after all! Turning it on I soon found that it accepted the passwords that I had always had for my laptop and decided to trawl the internet for what I could discover. I clicked on to the search engine. So what to look for first I wondered. I scanned the list that I had written in the notebook.

I knew I ought to start with Carna as she was the living breathing person that had entered my life, but afraid of what I might find I decided on Ovid as he had just appeared in our conversation. I typed his name into the search engine and copied out the information into my notebook. It read as follows:

'Publius Ovidius Naso (20 March 43 BC – AD 17/18), known as Ovid in the English-speaking world, was Roman poet who is best known as the author of the three major collections of erotic poetry: Heroides, Amores and Ars Amatoria. He is also well known for the Metamorphoses, a mythological hexameter poem; the Fasti, about the Roman calendar; although only the first six months of it are in existence today; and the Tristia and Epistulae ex Ponto, two collections of poems written in exile on the Black Sea. Ovid was also the author of several smaller pieces, the Remedia Amoris, the Medicamina Faciei Femineae and the long curse-poem Ibis. He also authored a lost tragedy, Medea. His poetry, much imitated during Late Antiquity and the Middle Ages, decisively influenced European art and literature and remains as one of the most important sources of Classical mythology. '

I decided that at some point I needed to have a good look at Carna's set of his works and that I was going to have to track down some English translations and read through them.

The next easiest name to look up had to be Janus. If he was a Roman God then there was bound to be stuff on him. I wondered if he was mentioned in Ovid's books.

Information about Janus soon appeared. The first thing that caught my eye was the picture of a statue of Janus which was identical to the bronze door knockers that adorned the front doors. The statue that was in the Vatican museum showed a two headed man. Each head had a long beard. Ringlets of hair hung down around his face with a long pony tail coming down behind his ears. Each head seemed to be a mirror image of the other although I could only see a side view. It was carved in white marble. I read the script.

'In ancient Roman Religion and mythology Janus is the god of beginnings and transitions, thence also of gates, doors and doorways, endings and time. He is usually a two-faced god since he looks to the future and the past. The concepts of January and janitor are both based on aspects of Janus.'

I wrote down the information and made a rather poor sketch of the statue. I wondered what that meant in terms of my situation. He was represented on the doors so there was a start. At present it was certainly a transition or new beginning or both. My future and past seemed totally disconnected at present.

I then scanned through the rest of the information it went on to describe cults, temples, rites and myths.

Frustrated with this mass of information I gave up and decided to try a different avenue. I entered Carna's name into the search engine and took a deep breath. To my surprise the information that appeared was about an island in Scotland that bore her name- Carna. I wondered if there was a connection but could not see what it could possibly be, unless it was to do with my sudden liking of Scottish whisky. I clicked on the information about the island. It did not have a distillery. I was certain that her name was important I was going to have to dig deeper.

Carna came to the door; guiltily I clicked on the delete button, not wanting her to see.

'Suppers ready.' She said and disappeared as quickly as she came. My research was going to have to wait.

I did not get time to get back on the computer that evening but after Carna had gone up to bed I went and had a look at her collection of books by Ovid. In front of the book shelf I was about to pull out one of the books, when I noticed a large black rock ornament about the size of a head adorning the top of the book case. Strangely I had not noticed this before. I was drawn to it and could not help myself from putting my hand upon its smooth surface. There was a flash of light and for a moment I felt as though all around me was bright light. I felt calmness and purity wash through me. It was like listening to the heartbeat of the earth, almost overwhelming in its intensity. I withdrew my hand and found myself standing before the book case once more. I looked round guiltily half expecting to see Carna behind me. I had an overwhelming urge to touch the stone again, but afraid I stepped back and sat down. Pulling my eyes from the stone I took a deep breath, forcing myself to focus on the books.

When I had a brief look earlier I had thought they were old but I got the distinct feeling that these were exceptionally old. Carefully feeling one of the pages with my fingers I was sure that it was not made of paper but of parchment. Parchment was used instead of paper from the time of Ovid up to the printing of the first book the

Guttenberg Bible in 1445. From then on virtually all books were made of paper. Parchment was a fine material made from the skin of an animal. The covers of the books looked more like the covers of old codices I had seen in museums. Then there was the writing. I could not read the Latin but there was no punctuation and it looked as if many of the words ran together. This suggested a very early piece of writing. I knew that punctuation and word separation came into use around the third and fourth century; which meant that this set of books must have been written around then or earlier meaning they were at least fifteen hundred years old. I let out a slow whistle at my discovery.

I pulled out my note book and made some notes. Then flicked through the books on the shelf to try and work out the titles. I wrote them down as I discovered them. As I wrote them I checked them off against the list that I had obtained from the internet. One immediately caught my eye and I pulled out the book to study it in more detail. At the top of the first page the title was clearly printed: *Medea.* I felt my heart beat faster and quickly checked my internet list where I had written '*He also authored a lost tragedy, Medea.*' This clearly seemed to be a copy of that lost book. If only I had learnt Latin I thought as I held the book and flicked through its pages.

I remembered one other comment about a part of a book being missing and flicked back through my notes. I read '*a mythological hexameter poem; the Fasti, about the Roman calendar; although only the first six months of it are in existence today*'. My hands shaking I searched through the books until I found the Fasti. Opening it up, I soon worked out that this copy went from Ianuarius, which I guessed was January to December. This collection had books that did not exist anywhere else. All my discoveries

I carefully entered into my notebook, writing a particular note to find out what I could about the large black stone, then put it deep into the back of the bottom drawer of the desk.

I headed upstairs, looking in on the sleeping Carna I went into the spare room. Surprisingly I fell asleep quickly. It was a fitful unquenching sleep full of dreams which were mainly of Carna and when I woke, feeling just as weary, I was still in the House.

V

The second of January was a work day so I was soon leaving the House. Climbing into the car, I felt the weight of the place drop from my shoulders and let out a sigh of relief, even if it was only to be for a short while. Plus going to work, I had the anticipation of discovering some more information from Geoff.

I arrived early. It was a cold morning; the office was chilly from little use over the New Year break. Rubbing my hands to warm them I went into the kitchen and put the kettle on.

Looking out across the office all was quiet, cold and still. My eyes rested on Geoff's desk. I had to go and look; I could not resist this early opportunity. My heart rate rose. Quickly I moved across the room and stopped at his desk. I stood listening for sounds or movement in the building but all seemed quiet, eerily so. I scanned the desk. There was a photo in a silver frame by the computer terminal. It had not been there before Christmas when I had looked in the desk with Lola. I picked it up; it was the picture of a young auburn haired woman holding a baby. I did not recognize her. Placing it carefully back down, I stopped for a moment listening again, and still all was quiet. I could not resist a quick look in the drawers where I knew that photo of Geoff's wife had once been. I was not surprised to discover that it was not there or in any of the other drawers that I could not stop myself rifling through.

At the sound of voices I quickly retreated to the kitchen and busied myself with making tea, trying hard not to show the guilt that I was certain must be written all over my face. It was not long before the door burst open and I heard a gaggle of laughing female voices entering the office which had to be Abigail and Lola. With a certain relief I called out;

'Good morning ladies, kettle's boiled.'

'Hi Francis, Happy New Year.' They both came over and hugged me. 'Did you have a good few days off?'

'Err, O.K., how about yourselves?' I replied quickly.

'Excellent. Party, party!' said Abigail swinging her arms. 'I feel as though I'm only just recovering.'

'Did you go out or stay in with that lovely wife of yours?' I wondered which wife she meant.

'Stayed in;' I retreated to my desk before any more questions came. I wanted to catch up with Geoff first. On an impulse I looked into the drawers of my own desk and with foreboding I pulled out an upside down picture frame in the bottom drawer. It looked identical to the one that we had previously discovered in Geoff's desk. I turned it over knowing what I would see and was not surprised to see a picture of Carna which looked as though it had come out of a modelling magazine. Quickly I dropped it back into the draw. It was early morning and already I was craving a drink of whisky.

Geoff did not appear all day. I had completed as much work as I was capable of but did not want to leave, especially without any more information. Lola was packing up her bag and pulling on her coat the rest of the office had already left. Carrying my cup on the pretext of washing it up in preparation to leave myself, I went over to her. I feared her response but had to say something.

'Have you seen or heard from Geoff at all?' I forced out as I stood watching her pull on her coat.

'Geoff?' I felt the bile rise in my throat. 'Oh Geoff!' she pointed across at his desk.' I felt a sense of relief' but it was short lived. 'What, since he left?'

'Left?' I stared at his desk.

'Well yes. It was this time last year wasn't it. Got that top job didn't he. He was well chuffed. Gosh I'd forgotten about him. Office has certainly been quieter since he left.' I wondered whether we were talking about the same person. The Geoff I remembered had been quiet as a church mouse and I had in fact only noticed him for the first time a couple of months ago. Sadly she had pointed to the same desk so I was certain considering the way things were at present that it was him. I wanted to bleat out that I had only seen him a few days ago and that he had been in the pub with us all not much more than a month ago. But I knew with a weary heart that there would be no point.

'Have you heard from him at all?' I said instead. 'It's only I fancy catching up with him. New Year's Resolution, you might say.' I added lamely, by way of explanation. 'You know, get in touch with people you haven't seen for a long time.'

'Good idea, that one. Better than mine; it's always to diet and I never get anywhere close to achieving it.' I smiled looking at her she did not need to lose an ounce of weight if anything putting a bit on might have helped but of course I did not comment. 'Now let me think… You know I don't think I have. Not even an email when he started the new job. I don't think anyone else did either. I remember Abigail asking about; after he had been gone a month and no one had heard anything.'

'Did he leave any forwarding information?' I said hopefully.

'Not with me. I don't remember Abigail finding anything either. She was going to contact him back then. I guess since then we've just forgotten and moved on, same as him I suppose. Looks like you're going to fail your New Year's Resolution too.' She laughed but the smile soon left her face as she watched me.

I could feel my heart pounding; I was breathing deeply. My anxiety and stress levels had finally reached melt down and it was beginning to have its affect. I was pale and felt clammy with sweat, my legs had turned to jelly and the rest of my body felt numb. I sat down on a nearby desk exhausted. All of a sudden I had not an ounce of energy or control over my body.

'Francis, are you ok?' I could feel Lola close to me but could not focus. I could hear the concern in her voice. I felt her pull me into a nearby chair. My head began spinning out of control, my thoughts full of conflict.

I could feel my previous life being slowly sucked away and was unsure what to do. This new life was filling its space. I tried to think of my wife and children. Their images seemed to be out of focus I struggled to see them clearly instead I saw Carna. Her image was slowly eroding and replacing them. With a sigh I allowed myself to collapse into an exhausted faint.

I woke to the sound of Lola calling my name. As my senses began to kick in I realized that I was lying on the floor. Lola was leaning over me. She was holding my hand.

'God! You had me worried Francis. I thought you were dead!' I looked up into her flustered face and felt myself smile. 'I'll get you a drink, do you want some water?' I nodded. My mouth was surprisingly dry and yet I felt clammy all over. I carefully sat up and leaned against the desk accepting the drink that she bought me I sipped it slowly. 'I'm going to drive you home ok.' She held her hand up to stop me interrupting. 'No complaints from you.

57

Plus you need to get to see a doctor ok? You've been over doing it.'

I certainly knew that was the case. I had not really slept properly since New Year's Eve and had spent the last two days in a high state of nervous tension. I was not sure how I would explain my situation to a doctor though. I staggered to my feet and realized that her offer of a lift was very sensible as I did not feel able to drive.

I soon found myself back at the House and tucked up in the master bedroom with Carna fussing around me. Strangely it did not feel uncomfortable. She produced a warm draught of dark coloured liquid. It smelled strange; a welter of aromas invaded my nostrils. It was like nothing my senses had come across before. She held it too my lips and bade me to drink; I took a sip, feeling its warmth sooth me as it travelled down my throat. Enjoying the myriad of flavours I gulped down the rest.

It had the desired affect within a short while I was in a deep dreamless sleep.

VI

I slept well into the next day. The deepest most comforting sleep I had had in many years. When I awoke I felt refreshed and calm. I could not remember what had been causing me so many problems. Carna said that I had become exhausted with the stress of work.

Visiting the doctor later in the day he signed me off work for a couple of weeks and told me I needed to relax and try to forget about work and any other worries I had for a while. If I did not feel better then he suggested I come back to him for some medication.

I was glad of the two weeks off but could not remember anything that had happened. I felt fine and had no memory of all that had gone before. When I discussed it with the doctor he said it may be amnesia brought on by stress and that it would eventually return. The fact that I had limited memory of anything before the previous day did not seem to worry me and every memory I did have was filled with Carna.

Everything seemed to be perfect. In my days off we walked together or I fished. I was catching so many fish that I was now just dropping them back in, the freezer was full. We swam in our pool. We went out for meals in the local pubs and restaurants and in the evenings we would sit and read by the fire. During the night we shared the master bedroom and each other as though we had done so for years.

I did not question the past, every time I thought about it I seemed to find myself thinking of and wanting Carna and she would suddenly be there and willing. Everything in this world of mine seemed naturally right as though it had carried on this way since the beginning of time. In fact time itself seemed to now have lost its meaning.

I returned to work in this state of strange euphoria and soon settled into a routine, wondering why I had become so stressed previously. I soon settled into the working life; A pattern that was to absorb me for many months. Everyone around me seemed to accept that this was and had always been the norm; not just my colleagues at work but friends and neighbours too. It was all too natural and easy for me to accept this situation as reality.

Indeed how could I not fall into this mental slumber. Whether Carna's interesting cocktails had anything to do with it; she liked to continue to prepare them for me in the evening; or the stress that I had suffered had caused me to block out the past. I was unsure later on, but having someone who always seems to know what you want, who is always there for you, who does not argue or complain, who's beauty makes men drool, makes it very hard to think that it is not right.

I sometimes wondered whether she was happy as occasionally when she smiled it was clouded by a certain sadness that seemed to radiate from deep within her soul, but she always denied that there was ever a problem when I questioned her.

So I sank into complacency and enjoyed living the moment. We began to discuss holidays. Maybe it was something in my subconscious but I was keen to go to Rome and upon my mentioning it Carna became excited; a youthful excitement that I had not seen her express before. She explained that she loved the city and its surrounding region and had visited when she was young, besides she said holding up the book she had been reading. 'I love

Ovid and he was Roman. Well born in Sulmona which is not far from Rome' she qualified. 'We could perhaps visit there. Where would you like to visit?'

'Got to be the Vatican,' I said. 'You see that place so often on the television. It's one of those few iconic buildings that is internationally famous. I fancy seeing the Coliseum to. That always looks like one impressive structure.' We had soon decided that this was to be our destination and began to surf the net for a prospective hotel.

It was Rome that started to cause me uncomfortable feelings about my present situation. We arrived on a warm spring day in March, quickly removing our wool jumpers, and took a taxi into the city. Carna's fluent Italian meant we had no problems.

Through the internet we had found a comfortable little hotel in the back streets near the Fonatana di Trevi. Our room was sparse, a brass bed and old fashioned dressing table plus a couple of hard chairs and small table by the long window. The floors were tiled and a fan hung above the bed. A door led to an en-suite that had not been refurbished since the fifties to my reckoning. It was all exceptionally clean and had a quaint old fashion feel to it. It felt like Rome.

Before we unpacked the excited Carna took me by the hand and said we must go and visit the Fountain. Clattering down the wide wooden stairway through the foyer, we were soon back out on the street. Tall renaissance style five story buildings towered up each side of us. The street was narrow and shaded but busy with people, tourists and locals moving intently in each direction.

'Come on this way.' Carna had my hand and pulled me along. Flushed and excited with her hair tumbling down her back and catching in the cool breeze blowing down the street she looked irresistible and I was soon affected by her excitement as she pulled me quickly through the narrow streets.

Suddenly the street opened up and we entered a large cobbled Piazza. Yellow and orange renaissance buildings on three sides but central and dominating the square was a large marble fronted palace ornate and symmetrical topped by a huge coat of arms. The building itself was impressive but the for-ground was what our eyes were immediately drawn to. For in a large alcove at the palaces centre stood a huge statue of Neptune atop watery winged horses and from beneath his feet and all along the base of the building a huge waterfall tumbled down into a clear sparkling pool of dancing turquoise water.

Finding a space at its edge I let my fingers run through its cool surface and lifting up a small handful I sprinkled it across my face feeling the exhausting effects of our journey evaporate. Carna laughed at me but also moved her hand through the water, almost caressing it lovingly. The gentle falling of the water seemed for a moment to hold back the noise and power of the city.

'I would just love to jump in and swim.' I muttered.

'If only we could. Naked and free as well.' Carna smiled at me teasingly. I felt my desire rising at the thought and implication. Trying desperately to change the direction of my thoughts I asked her to tell me about the fountain.

'This is the end point of an ancient aqueduct which brought pure water to Rome. The central figure is Oceanus also called Neptune. He rides a chariot pulled by two sea horses and guided by Tritons. One sea horse is calm the other is restive. The two faces of the sea.' At her mention of this I felt disturbed feeling there was something I should be able to remember which at present I could not quite grasp. She continued although I was now only half listening as I searched the recesses of my mind 'The statues either side of Oceanus are Abundance and Salubrity. It is a Baroque waterfall built into the existing face of the Palazzo Poli in 1726 by a Roman architect by the name of Nicola Salvi.' She looked at me 'Are you ok?'

'What oh yes. It's just that you reminded me of something but I can't quite remember what.' She looked at me with concern. 'You certainly know your history.'

Having had a meal in one of the many restaurants in the area we were soon back in our room laying on the brass framed bed side by side falling into an exhausted sleep. My mind was restless that night, whether it was lying in a new bed or it was Carna's words but they kept spinning around in my head. 'The two faces...the two faces...' I knew it was important but could not figure out why. As dawn rose I found myself sitting at the large window watching the early morning stirring of the Roman metropolis.

Over breakfast we discussed what we should do for the coming day. I was keen to visit the Vatican and its treasures. So we decided on a plan of action for the next few days. That day we would do the Vatican then the next we would visit the Roman part of the city including the coliseum. So with a couple of days at least sorted and a good breakfast inside us we took a taxi across the Tiber River to the Vatican City. Soon we were on the long approach road to the Vatican, the via Della Concilliazione. We got out of the taxi half way up and decided to walk the rest of the way. Ahead of us stood the grand St Peter's Basilica and St Peter's square. I was soon snapping away with my camera. Tourist buses jostled for position along the road disgorging their excited occupants. It was early but St. Peter's Square was already busy. We walked up to the central obelisk. Somehow it did not feel as big as it always looked on the television, when you saw it jam packed with the faithful waiting for the pope to appear. I decided though that it was just the fact that the Basilica was so dominant; it stood at the end of the square and drew the eye constantly, the huge dome towering up from behind the great ornate Roman façade. As we approached across the grey cobbles I felt I was being watched and judged by the marble saints that seemed to surround us on all sides, staring down from the tops of the colonnades and front of the Basilica.

Carna sat on the steps just outside; she said she had been round many times and would sit and wait while I wandered round.

Inside the heavy catholic Romanesque marble was overpowering. I found myself drawn to the delicate beauty of the Pieta by Michelangelo in the cool interior I studied the exquisitely carved features of the Madonna as she looked down upon the body of her dead son. I felt rooted to the spot and for a strange moment I was sure she turned her head and stared at me questioningly with her marble eyes that seemed somehow to exude passion and forgiveness. I was unnerved and felt my body shake. I could not hold that gaze feeling a sense of unworthiness and failure, I looked at the ground. When I looked up again all was as before and I wondered if I had been dreaming. I found myself questioning what is dream and what is reality, as I wandered round the rest of the great church, following the crowds to the central tomb of St Peter and staring up at the huge painted dome above. It was a question I was sure I had considered in depth before but found that I just could not quite remember. I was soon back at the huge doors and the bright sunshine outside.

I found Carna sitting on the steps watching the Swiss Guard in their antiquated uniforms. I sat down beside her. She put her arm through mine and I leaned back against the cool marble of the Basilica's grand façade. I was troubled by the Madonna's look. I felt certain it had happened but I reckoned even if it had not, my time there had left me uncertain and with a feeling I needed to look deeper. I gazed across the huge piazza trying to imagine it full of the faithful and found myself wondering about Carna. Turning to her I studied her beauty as she watched the guardsman with a smile just creasing the corners of her mouth' I noticed it created a small dimple in each of her cheeks.

'Why did you not come in?' she looked at me.

'Oh, I've been in before.'

'I know, you told me but that was a long time ago.' I still watched her searchingly, making her say more.

'Well, I guess I'm not religious.' She hesitated then qualified herself. 'Well not Christian anyway.' I had a strange feeling. Why had I not known this? Surely we must have got married in a church in England. We must have discussed this before but I had no memory of it or any clear picture of our wedding.

'Do you believe in anything?'

'The gods I suppose, especially here where we are surrounded by them.'

'Which gods?' she looked wistful although seeing back to a different age.

'Oh the Roman gods; you know Jupiter, Neptune, Mars, Venus.'

'Sounds like you're naming the planets.'

'Yes but important names to Rome of old that's why the planets are named after them; Jupiter-king of the gods, Neptune god of the sea, Mars god of war, Venus goddess of love. She's my favourite.' She finished squeezing my arm and resting her head on my shoulder.

'But why them? Aren't they a bit outdated somehow? I mean does anybody still worship them?'

'Oh I guess I just got connected to them.' She stopped, then added by way of clarification, 'through my studies; When I was learning Latin. Rome has always been my favourite subject. So I guess I just got attached to them.' She mumbled the last bit. 'Come on lets go to the museum.' I could tell she did not want to discuss it any more but I was not finished I needed to understand.

I could not forget the marble eyes of the Madonna boring into me questioningly, calling me to keep searching, for what I was as yet unsure but I now realised that somehow there were gaps that I needed to fill. I resisted the pull of her arm.

'Don't you think that they are somehow just a fractionalized God? If you put them all together you would have God. They are parts of the whole.'

'Yes I suppose you could say that.'

'Are they not just a way of humanising the unknown? You know, allowing us to put a face to it.'

'I guess you could say that too.' She stopped silent for a moment but I could tell she had not finished she was just thinking. 'Either way it is about inspiring us to look at ourselves and find our Inner Truth or strength, coming to terms with the unknown, whatever form we decide to accept.' We sat silently watching the crowds of tourists moving about animatedly around us.

'You know, I have no memory of us discussing anything like this before. Surely we talked about our faiths before?'

'You know your memory was affected at the New Year when you collapsed at work.' I nodded my mind working hard at this. Why had I not been more upset that I could not remember?

We got up and in contemplative silence which neither of us seemed ready to break we walked round to the queues for the Sistine Chapel. I must confess that I waited in the queue and followed the mass of people in there and hardly noticed the wonders that are there, my mind was in so much turmoil.

Of course like all the other tourists I picked out the spark of life from the hand of God but even this image unsettled me. It seemed to be calling for me to, well what? I just was not quite sure.

We wandered on along the Vatican wall to the Museum entrance. We had spoken little since our rest outside the Basilica. She had picked up my tension and I felt she feared its reason and broaching the subject in any way by breaking our silence.

Strangely, we entered the museum relatively easily, the queues not being too large. I found myself marvelling at the double spiral staircase that led up into the museum. Once inside we soon found ourselves deep in tourists. The bustle and excitement of this new place broke the ice and we were soon animatedly discussing a possible route through the maze of the museum.

We began to search out the treasures of the place using the guide book. It was difficult in the crowds;

Carna's Italian came in handy, especially as the labelling and directions were complicated. We had soon found famous artwork by Raphael and others. Indeed my senses soon became swamped by the powerful religious scenes. We moved on through other parts of the museum, feeling pulled along by the crowds stopping and looking at things that would suddenly grab our attention, Egyptian and Roman statues, bronzes, some amazing pieces of gold, wonderful ceramics and vases.

After some time I began feeling exhausted, my feet hot and aching. We decided to head for the exit. It was then that we stumbled upon a statue that I instantly recognized. I knew straight away that this was the reason I had entered the museum. I found myself like a rock in a river as the crowds swirled round me. The sculptured head stood before me on its plinth its two bearded identical faces looking out to the left and right. Janus drew me in. In my exhaustion I felt a mist of memories floating around me. I tried to focus on them but they just seemed out of reach. Images I was sure were of my past and yet in some I seemed older, perhaps to my future. Suddenly I saw the huge doors of my house before me. Through the one that we always used I saw Carna, smiling, insatiably beautiful. Then strangely the other briefly opened. I caught a glimpse of an auburn haired woman and two children. They were waving. I was sure I knew them but I just could not place it. Then as quickly the door was closed. I felt someone bump into me.

'Excuse' said a voice I stumbled forward feeling suddenly released, reaching out I placed my hand on the statue to steady myself. I heard a shout from a security guard and quickly let go. But not before I had felt the warm stone. It had felt alive like flesh. I was sure I had felt a pulse.

'Are you ok?' I heard Carna's voice as if in the distance growing louder as she repeated herself. I felt her holding me with an incredible strength as I was faint and unbalanced and hardly supporting myself. I gained my feet and nodded, pulling out a tissue I rubbed the sweat from my brow.

'Sorry, don't know what came over me.' The security guard came over and Carna placated him in her impeccable Italian. Still holding me she looked into my eyes.

'I feel confused Carna.' I looked at Janus. 'The gaps in my life; why am I not questioning them?' Turning back to her I noticed she too was looking at the statue, lost in thought. Her lips were moving quietly as if she was whispering to someone. It sounded like Latin. 'Carna?' I squeezed her hand.

'What? Oh, sorry I was distracted.' She looked back at the statue.

'He's doing it to you too.'

'How do you mean?'

'Well it was the statue here that disturbed me.' We stood contemplating it. The guard deciding that we were just slightly crazy tourists, walked off. 'Janus and his two faces,' I remembered the vision I had had. 'He is on our front doors, the door knockers. It made me think.' I turned her towards me and held her gaze. Not allowing her to look away. 'Why have we got two front doors? And why have I not questioned it before or even tried to use one of them.' She tried to look back at the statue. 'Oh come on Carna, you must know!' I raised my voice. I saw the guard once again looking in our direction. Carna flinched, unsure. Tears began to well in her eyes.

'I cannot tell you.' She muttered. She turned to the statue and spat out 'Videte quid faciatis!'

'What are you saying?'

'Oh nothing; Come on we are tired and arguing and we are meant to be on holiday.' She pulled me into the crowd and I did not get a chance to continue the conversation but I mentally noted down her words for a later translation.

We reached the spiral staircase in the atrium and headed down the downward spiral. A fascinating piece of architecture, it immediately got me thinking about all the doubles that were appearing. The two faces of Janus, the two doors to our house, even the two horses from the Trevi fountain these two entwined stairways, like the helix of DNA one from each parent male/female. As I walked down I thought of all the opposites, up and down, in and out, left and right, present and past, beginning and end, good and evil, dream and reality. The list was endless we could not seem to have one without the other; but what did it all mean to me?

Back at the hotel we collapsed on the bed together feeling the effects of our busy day. She reached out and held my hand.

'I am sorry Francis I cannot tell you, not yet anyway. Do not ask me.' She turned her head to me on the pillow, her eyes pleading. 'Do not stop looking for your memories, but do not ask me. I cannot help you, not yet. You will know when and then you will understand.'

Trying to stay calm, I said, 'Why? If you know something; I don't understand.'

'You will when the time is right. Please. It is better that you find out yourself rather than me tell you, then at least you will know it has come from your memory not mine.' She pulled me too her. 'We are on holiday.' She kissed me and soon I was forgetting my exhaustion and my confusion as I unbuttoned her blouse.

The next day I woke refreshed and did my best to put my doubts away for a while. After a slow breakfast we decided to walk to the Coliseum and the old Roman ruins around it. It was a refreshing walk through the waking city and we soon found ourselves in amongst the Roman ruins. The huge array of ancient crumbling buildings left me amazed. It took us all morning to walk through them, exploring where we could. Carna's knowledge of what each building was surprised me but I did not comment. Finally in the afternoon we found ourselves before the Constantine arch and the Coliseum.

As we explored its many layers I marvelled that such a construction could be built so that humans could enjoy the pain of others. It seemed to conflict with the other great building of Rome, the Vatican, on the other side of the Tiber which had been built, in theory at least, to promote faith and service to God. Once again the two faces of humanity stared at me. I thought if I was standing before the statue of Janus it would be smiling at me, with one of its faces at least.

The next few days flitted by. I had relaxed once again into the calm numbness that had possessed me before we had come away. We visited Sulmona the home of Ovid and I determined to read the books when I got back. In fact Carna challenged me.

It was on the last day of our holiday that we decided to head for the coast and the ancient Roman ruins of the

71

coastal town Ostia Antica, once the main port of Rome at the mouth of the River Tiber. We hired a car and drove. It did not take long and I soon found myself amongst the most amazing Roman ruins I had ever seen.

Ancient cobbled streets run through the city ruins, the building floors and squares carpeted with lush spring grass. Scattered Mediterranean cypresses, umbrella like, cover the area, creating a serene and tranquil mood.

I was impressed and I had only just stepped in through the entrance. I saw the excitement in Carna's eyes. She had become more animated than I could remember. She grabbed my hand.

'Come let me show you.' She pulled me down a cobbled street and I was soon lost amongst the grass carpeted ruins. She pointed out temples, piazzas, baths, the amphitheatre, markets even brothels. I saw mosaics, sculptures, proud pillars that once supported great buildings. As I watched and listened to her I felt as though she was there living it, hearing the voices and commotion, seeing the buildings in their entirety covered in marble. She made the place come alive to me.

Exhausted we collapsed on the steps of the Capitolium, the central government building, its red walls still standing proud reaching to the sky in proclamation. I watched a small lizard dart along the step below, sensing us it stopped its head lifted, eyes turned watching, totally still; its black yellow and brown flecks camouflaging it amongst the broken roman steps.

'Wow you certainly know this place.' She had a wistful far-away look in her eyes as she too studied the lizard.

'I grew up around here.' She muttered quietly. I took her hand.

'I should know that, shouldn't I?' once again I felt the overwhelming sense of fear and loss. I needed her to tell me something, even one small thing. 'Where,' I turned to her. 'Where did you grow up? Can you tell me that?'

She smiled at me nodding. 'Over there,' she pointed northwards, 'Across the Tiber. It's a place called Isola Sacra.'

'And what does that mean?' After some hesitation she translated.

'The Sacred Isle.'

We sat silently for moment as still as the lizard.

'I thought we might go there.' She turned her gaze full upon me. The sun glinted in her deep blue eyes; her dark hair glistened with impressionistic colour. She looked stunning. She took my silence for hesitation. 'If you don't mind that is.' I shook my head. Suddenly a further thought, a need to know, sprang into my mind.

'Do you have family here?' I was strangely excited at the prospect of meeting in-laws and other family members. She soon deflated me with a shake of the head. 'Shame, I would have liked to meet them. Do you have any family?' she shook her head again. Now not looking at me but lost in the past, enveloped in a pale sadness. I dared not push her with further enquiries. I decided to focus back on the present.

'Ok then… I'm guessing this here is probably the most impressive ruin left but which is your favourite? Which one draws you back to it?'

'Magna Mater.' She said quickly without thought, then pausing to reflect. 'Yes I guess, Cybele. The Campo Della Magna Mater, the Great Mother goddess of fertility and nature. Her story is in my Ovid.' Once again she fell silent; as she thought, the speckled lizard watched us its

73

dark pupils with their orange circumference fixed upon us. 'Plus this of course' she continued 'the Forum Capitolium dedicated to the triad Jupiter, Juno and Minerva, and I guess the many Nymphaea, the springs with their shrines, a Nymph is a supernatural female being often associated with water and springs.'

I patted her leg 'Come on then let's go have a look at this house of the Great mother goddess and then we'll see if we can find our way to your Sacred Isle. What was that called again the Isole Sac...?' She took my hand and laughed.

'Almost, the Isola Sacra.' I stood up pulling her after me.

'Come on then; which direction?'

'That way' she said pointing east. 'I warn you there's not much there.'

'And yet it's your favourite?' I looked at her questioningly she looked away hesitantly.

'I have no family.' She turned her hair flying round, silky in the sun, her wide bright eyes held my gaze. I felt weak. She seemed to possess me with her gaze. I felt my will to rebel, to search out truth evaporate. I felt as though her will was mine and I should not question it. 'I like to think of her as a mother figure, my mother figure.' She continued, 'No family you see...' Her eyes seemed to search my soul. I just nodded, when actually I had so many questions. We walked hand in hand through the ruins. I shook my head and sipped from my water bottle.

'Sun's hot' I mumbled wondering if I was just suffering from sunstroke 'I can't believe it's just the end of March. It's like a summer's day'. We soon entered a clearing, triangular in shape, edged by huge Corsican pines creating shade which I gratefully walked under. Carna led

74

me to a corner and pointed to ten aged steps that led up to an over grown wall. It felt strangely tranquil, safe; full of presence.

'The Temple of Cybele,' she said simply. Releasing my hand, she headed up the steps her head bowed. I followed her stopping on the third step, which was larger than the rest containing a small landing, fearing to go further, I watched Carna disappear into the ruin. Finally steeling myself to move forward I walked up the remaining marble steps. Through the remains of the plant covered brick structure I could see Carna kneeling at the far end. She seemed to be praying or meditating. I did not want to disturb her. So I watched her for a moment then turned to look across the grass covered court yard, dappled in sunlight. I tried to imagine it full of life, the devout Romans moving about their business, coming across the court yard to the temple. I felt a hand slide into mine.

'Thank you'

'What for?'

'Giving me a moment'

'We each need a place.' I said vaguely. She nodded. Her eyes glistened. I wiped away the start of a tear. 'Come lets go find the Sacred Isle.'

We clambered into the sweltering hire car quickly opening the windows. We stuck our heads out into the cool air that rushed in as we set off. We were soon heading out of Ostia.

We took a right turn onto the Fiumicino road. This was the town that now spread across much of the Island. The road crossed the Tiber. I slowed to get some views up and down the river to the consternation of the cars behind, who hooted as they tried to pass. It was a slow flowing river; its dark waters sparkling in the sun. A few small boats meandered lethargically along. Then as suddenly as it had appeared it was gone and we were onto the Sacred Isle.

'Ok' I said turning to her as we cruised slowly along. 'Here we are, but where too now?'

'The tombs, I guess.' She waved her hand vaguely. 'It is all so populated now.' She grunted, annoyed, 'and look at all these advertising boards along the road. How ugly. There was a time when the whole area was wild and beautiful; woodlands of Holm Oak and Corkwood Pine, vast areas of scrub called Macchia, made up of Rosemary, Thyme, Lavender, Juniper, Broom and Heather. The scent was heavenly.' She sighed.

We came up to some traffic lights. 'I hate to bring you back to the present but which way?'

'Go across; head for that white water tower.' We drove on up the road lined with modern buildings. 'Here turn right just after those traffic lights past the tower.' I followed her instructions.

'Via Cima Cristallo.' I murmured, reading the sign. I turned.

'Left there,' she said pointing after a few hundred metres. 'That will take us to the Roman tombs, The Necropoli di Porto.' I dutifully followed her instructions; finally pulling up next to two flag poles bearing the Italian and euro flags. A gate to our right led through a high fence topped with barbed wire into the site.

'Not too busy here.' I commented. We were the only car. 'At least there will be some shade under those huge pines.'

Inside we came across a smiling caretaker who chatted away animatedly to Carna. I wandered off amongst the ancient tombs as she paid; musing as I went at the fact that she had lived here and known it so different. She was not much older than I was, or so I thought any way, and the streets outside must have been about when I was young some twenty years before; Another piece of my most confusing puzzle.

The large number of huge tombs were scattered along a road. Small tracks weaved between them. It looked like a small ruined town. I was hot; the heat had sucked the energy from me and I felt slightly exhausted by more red brick ruins so I headed for some huge shady pines that bordered the site; waving at Carna as I sat down. She signalled that she was going for a wander; not feeling like following her I gave an extravagant nod to show I understood and settled down on the dry warm grass with a sigh. The air quivered with heat above the ground and buildings.

I lay back and enjoyed the shade. Closing my eyes, I listened to the hum of insects, the occasional call of a bird, the whispering of the gentle breeze and the continuous hum of traffic in the distance. It was not quiet but the world for a moment was still and I enjoyed its peace.

It did not last long; soon my doubts crept in, the unknowns that seemed to fill every corner of my existence. I wondered if I was in a dream and knew I had had this thought before. It all felt real but somehow I doubted reality.

Hearing a sound I sat up suddenly. It was the sound of children playing. Lifting my head up, I saw them darting amongst the ruins, two of them, their mother laughing and chasing them, her auburn hair flashing in the sun. I knew them; I knew that I knew them. They were the same family I had seen as I stood before the statue in the museum. The woman turned and looked directly at me she lifted her hand, I raised mine without thinking and was about to call out.

'Francis, Francis, are you all right?' Turning I saw Carna approaching. I felt annoyed and turned back quickly but the children and the woman had gone. Carna came up to me. 'What is it?' she knelt beside me concern in her eyes. 'You are very pale. Are you ok?'

'What? yes!' I snapped 'Course I am,' although I did feel dizzy and lay back down on the grass. 'Just a bit of sunstroke that's all.'

'You must have some of my tonic when we get back. You have not had any since we got to Rome.' At the mention of it I could sense my taste buds beginning to salivate, my brain willing me to accept. I was unsure why I had constantly refused her offers since we landed in Rome but something about coming here had caused me to say no and our busyness meant that I had not had time to dwell upon it. The image of the two children and the woman were imprinted on the eyelids of my closed eyes. I felt Carna take my hand and squeeze it but I knew I must refuse her.

'No I don't need it now. The shock following my collapse at New Year is long gone. I am healthy and fit. I just need to find myself and I don't think your tonic helps me with that.' I opened my eyes and watched her. An expression of distress or could it be annoyance flicked across her face and was as quickly gone.

My head had started to pound and I would have liked some tablets but I was determined not to let on and give her another excuse to tempt me with her elixir. So I sat up. 'How was your walk round?'

'Interesting,' she looked up at a bird of prey screeching as it circled lazily in a thermal above. 'Not the same but there you are, nothing ever is.'

'Time does not stand still.' She smiled at me.

'I found a lovely mosaic of Venus. I came back to get you.'

'Ah your favourite goddess;' we visited her mosaic in one of the tombs. I was no longer the best of company and my mood soon transmitted to Carna, so it was not long before we were heading back to Rome in the car.

VII

During the journey back to England we said little to each other both of us lost in our thoughts. Carna seemed sad at having to return. I felt confused. I was even more determined now to find my lost memories. I realised that for some time I had thought little about it and just lived, going from day to day without questioning. I felt agitated and unsettled but felt that I must not succumb to Carna's relaxing tonic.

The air was cold as we stepped off the plane and drove to the house. Carna had sunk into herself and did not want to come out of her reverie. It was unnatural and unnerved me. I also did not want to speak because I was certain she would not answer what I wanted to know.

We arrived at the house late in the evening; Carna quickly disappeared inside, leaving me facing those two front doors. I stood before them holding our suitcases. It was not until Carna, wondering where I was returned and called me in that I moved. I determined that I would have a good look at that other door in the morning.

Feeling an increasing weight on my shoulders, I sighed and stepped slowly into the hallway. After a quick bite to eat with Carna in the kitchen, a thrown together sandwich and some soup, Carna headed off to bed. I realised that it was not often that I had found myself alone in the house and although I felt exhausted too, I determined to stay up, to think and try to get my head round my strange feelings. I did not think I could sleep anyway, which was to become a recurring problem as time went on. Heading into the lounge I poured myself some of the whisky which had become my favourite and from what I had been told had always been so.

Standing in the centre of the room I sipped contemplatively. I stared at the cold empty hearth. It seemed to observe me back, a sightless stare if such a thing could exist. It made me shiver and I began to pace. After a while I pulled out some of Carna's books by Ovid. Strange I thought that I could not remember ever looking at them before and yet they seemed so old and beautiful. I opened one reverently; the parchment crackled. They appeared to be hand written in scrawling Latin.

My mind reeled at the confusion of my reality. I seemed to have everything and yet, I could not place my finger on it. It just did not feel right, sort of dreamy and the more I fought it the more agitated I found myself.

Filling my whisky glass and carrying the remainder of the bottle with me, I wandered into the study. I had not been in here for a long time I realised. Slowly I moved round the book shelves; line upon line of fascinating novels, non-fiction, reference books, and excellent antique books in perfect condition. Every one of them was a book that I would have bought if I had seen it and had the money and yet I had no recollection of any of them.

I shook my head angrily, I must have bought them in the past, and it was just my memory loss from my collapse at New Year. Downing my whisky I headed off to sleep.

I slept little and dreamt a lot, waking in the same agitation I had got into bed with. In contrast, Carna woke refreshed and seemed to be her old self. She tried to get me to swim and refresh myself but I stubbornly refused, retreating into silence, I did not even want to wash or shave. After a strong coffee, whilst Carna swam I went out of the door and stood at the front of the house. We always used the left door, I moved closer studying the left and the right in turn; they were identical. Of course I already knew this. The faces of Janus stared back at me. I turned the handle on the right hand door. It turned but the door was securely locked. I could not remember a key.

After a moments contemplation I took the key from the inside of the left door and put it in the right hand door. It fitted perfectly and turned; the lock seemed well oiled and in perfect condition as though it was used every day and yet I had no memory of it ever being open. I turned the handle and yet the door still did not open. I went inside to see if it had any hidden bolts but none were there. I turned the handle from the inside, still no movement. I felt my anger levels rising and standing back I gave it a massive kick, it did not budge. I kicked again and again but nothing. Running out of the house I went into the garage and came back with a sledgehammer. I realised I was smiling as I lifted it and swung it at the door.

It did not even dent it. I swung again and again, throwing all my frustrations into every blow, sweat began to course down my back and across my brow but nothing, not a mark. I went outside and tried the same even turning my attention to the Janus doorknocker when I had failed totally to mark or move the door. Tears of frustration came to my eyes. Janus stared back; he seemed to be laughing at me. I threw one final giant blow at the top of his head and heard the shaft of my sledgehammer crack.

I collapsed onto the step my hands stinging and blistered from my failed exertions. A dog barked and I looked up to see an old couple standing on the pavement with a small white scotch terrier pulling at the lead as it tried to reach me. Quickly they turned away and began to walk as fast as their old legs would allow them, pulling the barking dog along behind them. I laughed, an angry confused and bitter laugh, torn from me. A sound behind me made me turn. There stood Carna, wet and beautiful, partially wrapped in a small towel fresh from her swim. She just stood and watched me, anxiety in her eyes. I stood up, holding the sledgehammer in my hands. I noticed a twinge of fear in her; I looked at it and the door then back to her.

'Bloody door, no key seems to open it. Can't even dent it with this no matter how hard I try.'

'I was wondering what all that noise was.' She came over and took the sledgehammer, propping it in the corner of the room. 'Door's always been like that. Only opens when it wants to.' I picked up on that.

'So it has opened then? In the past I mean.' She nodded, 'When?'

'Last time it was open was once over Christmas. Just before...'

'Yes, I know.' I said irritably, 'Just before I lost my memory.' As I looked at her I could feel my desire getting the better of me. So I turned and stormed out of the front door that was still open.

I walked for miles. Returning exhausted in the afternoon, I crashed onto the sofa.

I staggered through work that week, in a state of nervous dishevelled exhaustion. Everything made me tense. My anxiety levels rose with each dawn. After such a holiday I knew I should feel good and relaxed but somehow I found myself unable to settle. Thoughts of what my past was like constantly unsettled and puzzled me, plus somehow my present just did not seem right. It did not ring true but I could not put my finger on why. So each day I grew more ragged and irritable. Until in the second week I found I just did not have the energy or willpower to go to work. I hid myself away in the spare room and refused to speak when Carna came in and attempted to entice me up.

Later that morning Carna returned and said that she had made me an appointment at the doctors and that I should go at 3.00pm. I grunted back in return saying that I did not need to go and I just needed to get my head together. I heard her leave the room and eventually a little while later I heard the front door go. The house sank into silence and I sat up disturbed by the sudden quiet and feeling of emptiness within the house, it seemed to mirror my feelings. I gave a hollow laugh which seemed to echo.

I slowly wandered the house in my boxer shorts, my mind a place of confused thoughts, which shot in and out of it randomly. I eventually ended up in the kitchen and poured myself a coffee from the machine. Slowly I talked myself into visiting the doctors, knowing that at present I could not see the wood for the trees and was just going round in circles.

The doctor listened patiently as I rambled on about the inconsistencies of my reality and my not remembering any of my past. He nodded sagely at regular intervals. When I finally dried up, he pronounced his diagnosis of depression caused by my memory loss and prescribed me a course of anti-depressants and referred me to a counsellor. He also signed me off work for three months.

'Time and rest is what you need. It should all come back slowly and as you gain your memory then you will feel more connected to your present.' He patted me on the back as he guided me to his door, 'you will see, mark my words.'

The tablets numbed my thoughts and allowed me to appear to function on the surface that subdued the raging chaos below. It meant I was able to get out and our lives returned to some normality. Most days I swam, walked and fished.

After a few weeks I had my first appointment with the counsellor, a middle aged rather large woman, her grey hair tied back. She had sharp piercing eyes that seemed to look right into me. I sat opposite her and slowly with prompting opened up to her, although I was a bit reserved about my strange thoughts about Janus and Carna and said little on these. I had in fact not mentioned them at all to the doctor. As with the doctor she nodded and listened, also stressing the link between my memory loss and my feelings of lost reality. Saying that without a past to base it all on it was hard to hold down what was happening around me. She agreed that the family I was seeing was probably connected to my past in some way and that it may be useful to find them to help. She was perplexed at the fact that Carna seemed unable to help me regain my past. She suggested I write things down and try to get some order into my feelings. Plus that I search for memories through things at the house. She was certain that there must be objects, letters, notes, photos in the house that will help trigger my past. I left feeling as though I had a direction and said I would return the following week. I was determined in the interim to find at least something. I realised that understanding my situation hinged on my finding some memory of before January.

I returned to the house, refusing to look at the door knockers. Carna was out so I began a massive search of the house, delving into every corner of every room, searching the attic, the sheds, the garage. Finally exasperated, I collapsed at the desk in the study, the inevitable whisky glass in my hand and bottle on the table. I had searched high and low but found nothing that could help me see further back than my collapse.

Nothing in the house seemed to stir any kind of memory. The study was the only room left. My eyes roved around the room, desperately, taking in the books the photos on the desk of myself and Carna. There appeared to be nothing. Even when I picked up and studied the photos, I could not remember where they had been taken. I banged the desk angrily feeling my agitation return. I breathed deeply and told myself to keep searching. I began to empty the three drawers of the desk one at a time and tipped the contents out in front of me. The first one contained stationary and paper but there was not a single written word. The second contained bills and financial information connected to the house. I had often used these first two but the last one I realised I had not opened for some time, in fact I thought excitedly I had no memory of opening it. I pulled it out and tipped it on the table. It contained a dictionary, a thesaurus, train time table, a booklet outlining what's on at the theatre, and a small notebook.

I picked it up and opened it. I instantly recognised my own hand writing. I realised it was the first piece of handwriting that belonged to me that I had seen that dated to a time before my collapse. Nervously I read:

1. *As I have not returned to my previous existence I must assume that I am in some sort of reality. A place that I must at least come to terms with and perhaps live in forever. If I can!*

2. *Everything had changed when I arrived with Geoff at his house. Note-need to find Geoff.*

3. *What does Janus have to do with all this? Note -research Janus.*

4. *Who is Carna? Why did she appear different to me? Why will she not tell me what has happened? I am sure she knows. Why did she say you must know when to ask me?*

5. *The House. Why two front doors?*

6. *What happened to my family? Why did Rosie's parents say she had died when she was young?*

7. *Above all hold on to the memory of Rosie, my wife and my children Theresa and Michael*

8. *What is special about Ovid or his books?*

9. *Is Rome, Latin important? It seems to be to Carna.*

I sat back in the chair stunned at the enormity of what I was reading. It meant that I had been confused about my situation before my collapse. There was no date but it gave me plenty to contemplate and some starting points in my search. I realised there was more in the small notebook and read on. Discovering the information on Ovid and Janus, his statue that we had seen in Rome, there it was in the notebook, a poor sketch in my own hand. I scanned the notes on the Ovid texts and the fact that Carna's set contained missing books, plus the mention of a large stone ornament on the bookshelf. Strange I thought I could not remember that. I read of my visit to Rosie's parents and what they had said, of my visit to the Geoff's house and the fact that he did not actually live there anymore. There were in fact notes on everything that had happened since the works get together before Christmas up until my collapse.

I sat back exhausted and confused. The words 'Rosie my wife and my children, Theresa and Michael', still reverberating round and round in my head. Somehow I was certain this was the family I had seen in Rome. It was a memory; the one memory that I had. I wondered if this meant I had been married before and something terrible had happened, which was the reason for my blanking out my past.

I heard the door go which jerked me back into the present. I quickly pushed the notebook into the back of the draw where I had found it. One question filled my head and I moved to intercept Carna before she could even find me. I surprised her in the hall removing her boots. She turned and smiled but I could not smile; I just had to know. I pulled her up rather roughly and turned her to me holding her by the shoulders. I could feel her concern but I could not stop myself.

'Carna, I need to know.' She smiled at me nervously. 'I need to know if I was married before.' She looked confused now. 'You know, before us.'

'I don't want to talk about the past. I have told you before.' In my agitation I began shaking her.

'But surely, this! It's just a yes or a no!' I was shouting now. 'It's not about you!' She pulled away from me.

'I have told you before.' Her voice was raised too, which surprised me as she had always remained calm. 'I cannot; I am not allowed, not able to tell you.' She pushed past me and walked down the hall.

'Thank you!' I spat out. 'That is just going to make me worse; make me want to know more!' at that she stopped and turned.

'I want to tell you.' There were tears in her eyes. 'I want so much to explain.' Her voice became quiet almost a whisper. 'Each time it's torture.' She was shaking her head. I stepped forward, towards her, craning to catch her words. 'There is just one day when I am free; free to speak. Find that day.' There was desperation in her voice. I was about to speak but she held up her hand. 'I cannot say any more. Search by all means, when you know you will understand.' She was shaking now. I found myself moving towards her, holding her. 'I wonder sometimes if it would be better not to know or understand and just live and enjoy that life we have been given.' She looked up at me hopefully.

For a moment I did not know what to think; what to do. She was mesmerising in her perfection, even with tears running down her face, I found myself just wanting to hold her, wipe her tears away, forget my confusion and make her happy. I felt myself succumbing. I tore my eyes from her face and looked up over her shoulder. I was looking into the hall mirror which reflected back an image of the two of us and behind us those doors. It brought me back with a jolt and I pulled away.

'If this was where my past had brought me then I could, will, be happy. But I must find that past.' My conviction was once again strong. 'I have to; I cannot be happy until I can tie all the loose ends of my life together.' A resigned look came over her. 'I am sorry.' She nodded.

'I understand and I wish I could help you.'

'Why can't you?' I felt my anger rising. 'I just cannot understand why you can't.' she just shook her head.

'It must be your journey. I am here for you but it must be your journey.' She let go of me with an audible sigh. 'I will make some tea.'

'Not for me.' I said turning back towards the study via the lounge where I grabbed the inevitable whisky bottle and glass before retreating into the study.

I sat, pulled out the note book and went over the conversation. Something Carna had said had confused me but in my anger I had not picked up on it. I poured my whisky and sat back in the chair, holding the glass of golden nectar, swilling it slowly and sipping contemplatively, my heart rate slowing. Then I had it. I picked up a pen and opened the little notebook deciding to add more notes to those already there. I wrote.

Why was she not able to tell me?

Why was she not allowed and by whom?

What does she mean by each time its torture?

I put the pen down and sat back. There were so many questions and yet few answers. Where should I begin? I was at a loss, floundering about in something bigger than my poor human mind could comprehend.

I needed a plan. I needed to work at something that was easy to grasp. Janus and Ovid, the doors, Rome, that was all something too woolly to get my head round. I decided it was the people in my life that was where I needed to start, Carna, Rosie and Geoff. I felt sure that through them I could find answers. Carna would not tell me. The notes said Rosie was dead and had died young. Geoff had disappeared.

Filling my glass again I flicked on the computer, finding the search engine I entered CARNA and held my breath. There was the Scottish Island that I had discovered before. There was also a reference to a town called Carna in Ireland these places may be important but other references such as to an association of nurses I felt I could rule out straight away. I clicked on the link to the free encyclopaedia. Once again I saw mentions of the Scottish island and the small town in Ireland then under the title-Other, I was sure I had hit the jackpot. I felt my heart rate increase as I read on excitedly and quickly copied down the information.

'*An ancient roman deity, whose identity became confused with Cardea.*' I clicked on Cardea which was highlighted and nearly fell off my chair with what appeared. I gulped at my whisky and wrote down the following in my little book. '*Cardea was the ancient Roman Goddess of the Hinge. Roman doors being hung on pivot hinges. The Poet Ovid conflates her with another archaic goddess called CARNA whose festival was celebrated on the Kalends of June and for whom he gives the alternative name of Cranea, a nymph.*' The words Roman, doors and Ovid jumped out at me. I underlined them. Carna was a goddess, Janus a god. That too, I was certain was important and scribbled down a further note. I remembered the goddesses on the door hinges on our front doors. They had to be representations of Carna. I was getting information but could not understand how any of this could possibly be connected in any way.

That was as far as I got that day and I made no further progress before my next counselling session.

'So you found a notebook that told you that things weren't right before you lost your memory.' The counsellor looked at me over her glasses, a little confused. I nodded. She continued summarising as I sat opposite her, 'a book that mentions that you had a wife called Rosie and um children.'

'Yes that's right called Michael and Theresa.' She looked at me silently. I guess I did not look so good. I was becoming so wrapped up in this that I was forgetting my personal hygiene and grooming. It was beginning to show. I was getting quite a growth of beard and my hair was uncombed and unwashed. I found myself patting it down with my fingers. I was suddenly conscious of my scruffy clothes, although at the time it just did not seem to matter.

'Do you have it with you, this notebook?' I shook my head. I had not wanted to bring it for fear she would think I was going crazy if she read through all that was in it. Now I began to wonder if she was thinking that any way. 'Will you bring it next time?' I vaguely nodded conveying a yes, maybe, maybe not. 'And Carna will not say anything about this?' I shook my head again. 'Perhaps you could bring her with you next time.'

That seemed like a good idea I thought someone else questioning her instead of me. I agreed to do my best to get her to come. She stood holding out her hand and I realised my time was up. She had a firm grip and held on for a moment studying me once again.

'You are continuing to take your medication regularly are you?' I assured her that I was, but at the same time had a niggling doubt that she was not taking me seriously.

That night I dreamed.

I was steering the narrow boat into the lock. A woman, the woman, was smiling back at me. She had just pushed open the lock gate with a small girl. A boy on the other side was jumping up and down excitedly.

'I did it! I did it!' he was shouting excitedly. 'I told you I could push it open on my own!' The boat entered the lock and they closed the gates behind it and all ran up to the other end racing each side of the lock shouting and laughing.

'Beat you!' shouted the girl across to her brother.

'Not till you've opened the lock;' he said urgently, fitting the lock key into the gate.

'Come on mum!' shouted the girl to the woman. 'Quick he's going to win!' Soon the boat was rising as the water rushed in. 'Dad!' the girl was looking at me. 'It's not fair, mum's going too slowly!' The woman smiled back at me as she cranked the handle just slow enough to allow the boy to win. He was jumping up and down.

'Dad'll get you on the next one.' She called across at him. She stepped on the boat as it came up and reached across to me; pulling my head down and kissing me. 'Your turn now darling I'm pooped.'

'Yeah come on dad, we'll beat him!' the girl was shouting. I jumped up onto the bank; I ran, laughing as I went.

Passing the bow of the boat, the dark water from the lock bubbling around it, I found myself staring at its name and the two faced bearded image carved into its prow. I stopped and stared at the name emblazoned across the bow in gold letters. I was screaming, shouting out the name, repeatedly.

'*JANUS!* JANUS!'

My vision filled now just by the figure head and the name beneath it. Suddenly that too became hazy and then there was just darkness; the word Janus echoing around the deep empty space. I found myself shouting 'no!' as I burst out of the dream into this unreal, real world, damp with sweat.

I turned to find Carna siting up in bed watching me. 'Are you ok?'

After a moment to settle my racing heart and erratic breathing I nodded.

'Just a dream.' I swung my legs out of bed and got up; the dream still fresh in my mind.

'Come here,' she beckoned me forward. 'Get back in.' I was drawn by her. Her face pale in the moonlight that was sneaking through the curtains, her eyes seemed to suck the resistance out of me. She was so impossible to refuse. I sat down on the edge of the bed intending to get back in but the moment I broke her gaze, the dream was back.

'No' I said without looking round at her 'I just need a moment.'

'Where are you going?' Her voice rose concerned at her failure.

'Just down stairs; don't panic.' I was soon in the study with the inevitable whisky bottle pacing up and down, replaying the dream.

I pulled out the little notebook and began to write, replaying the dream; I was sure it was real, a memory. I was now determined to trace them, even if the notebook said that they did not seem to exist. I decided I needed to visit the address that was written in the notebook that was supposedly her parents.

My plan made; I had some time to kill before I could go door knocking so, not wanting to be in the house when Carna came down, I picked up my fishing gear and walked down to the lake as the dawn came up.

It was a beautiful dawn the sun crawling up and battling with darting clouds. The birds became ecstatic with the promise of a new day, outdoing each other with their song. My grogginess slipped away as I waded out into the water and cast. The orange glow flashed in the ripples, dancing in and out of shadow. I knew I would catch, I always did now. In fact I had not fished for a while as the adventure had gone out of it. It did not seem to matter how badly I fished, I caught. As I reeled in the first one, a strong sleek healthy two and a half pound Brown Trout, I determined to write a note in the book about this strange success that I seemed to have.

I held the fish for a moment, it gaped for air. I could not take its life. Nature was too prevalent that morning. It somehow did not feel right. I lowered it down into the water and watched as, for a moment it stayed still dazed and exhausted, its wide left eye stared up at me, and then with a thrust of its tail it disappeared.

For four hours I caught and gently released fish. I did not even count them, just allowing the rhythm to take over, emptying my mind of everything but the moment; letting the sound of the waking world wash over me.

At last I was ready to go. I felt tired but refreshed. After a quick shower and some coffee and toast I headed out in the car leaving a worried looking Carna on the door step. I reached the address after about forty minutes and stopped on the street outside. I looked around searching my memory for clues. I knew if I had been married to Rosie I must have visited this place regularly but I could not find anything.

Getting out of the car I walked through the gate and into the small driveway. Hearing a shout I looked across onto the front lawn. A boy was playing football with two men. He was laughing as he dived on the ball then picked it up and threw it. I found myself rooted to the spot. Both men turned; their eyes following the ball. Neither of them seemed to notice me. The older man I did not know. But the younger man I did.

'I'll get it Harry!' he called across at the grey haired man. 'Harry,' I thought remembering my notes, 'Rosie's father.' My eyes were glued to the younger man, for I knew him well. I stood and watch myself pick up the ball and kick it up in the air for the young boy to catch. 'Great catch Michael!' I heard myself shout.

I heard the sound of the front door opening and turned to see that same grey haired man looking out at me. Turning back quickly to the lawn I found it empty and quiet, not a mark in the fresh morning dew that covered the grass.

'Can I help you?' said the man who I now knew was Harry. He seemed to recognise me. 'You!' he said angrily. 'What do you want?' I was speechless. I just did not know where to start and just found myself staring at him. 'You upset us enough at New Year. My wife…' He stared back at me unnerved by my silence.

'I'm sorry.' I said 'it's just that I need some information. You see some time ago I lost my memory.' I was unsure how to continue. Words that I had planned on my way over had been lost with the site of the strange vision on the front lawn. 'I'm sure some how you were part of my past; Rosie too. I'm just trying to work it out. I don't mean any harm.' I noticed a lady standing in the shadow just inside the door. Harry was looking nervous.

'No we can't help you.' He said. He went to close the door.

'Wait! Harry let's hear him out.'

'But…'

'It can do no harm and if it helps him then well that can only be to the good.' Harry hesitantly stood back.

'You had better come in then' I followed Matilda into the kitchen. I sat down nervously for I did not quite know how to start.

'She would be about your age now' said Matilda as she filled the kettle, her back to me. Harry stood at the door fidgeting. She switched the kettle on and faced me. In her face I recognised the woman I had seen. 'When you came before you said you were her friend. I knew her friends. What is your name?'

'Francis, Francis Smith.' I held my breath, hoping, but after a moment she just shook her head.

'No, it does not ring a bell.' She recognised my disappointment. 'You say you have lost your memory?' I explained that I had collapsed not long after seeing them and only knew that I had visited because of a note in a small note book that I had recently found. Harry coughed. I had forgotten he was there as I talked.

'What did it say?' He asked coming and sitting down. Matilda poured out the tea from a china teapot and sat too. I pulled the book from my pocket; unsure whether it was a good idea to show them.

'Some of what it says you might find very strange.' I read the few sparse notes of my last visit. And then number six and seven from the list:

6.   *What happened to my family? Why did Rosie's parents say she had died when she was young?*

7.   *Above all hold on to the memory of Rosie, my wife and my children Theresa and Michael*

'That's crazy' muttered Henry 'Rosie your wife. She was twelve when it happened.'

'I don't understand. why would you write that?' I shook my head.

'I don't know but I need to try to work it out. I think it's important, a clue.' I almost told them of my dreams but held back certain that they would not cope with that. 'If you feel able to tell me...' I paused trying to find the words. Matilda nodded understanding

'You would like to know what happened to Rosie.' It was my turn to nod.

They looked at each other. Harry took Matilda's hand.

'She just went up the shop; to get her magazine.' He said his voice weak and faltering. Matilda's eyes began to glisten. She squeezed his hand. 'It's not far. Just up the road, then you cross over. It's on the other side, you see.' He stopped and looked away, staring out of the window. Matilda carried on.

'She was hit crossing over. A hit and run. Car just carried on. A big silver thing, Italian they think. A man coming out of the shop got the number plate. Only...' she fell silent. I dared not speak, so just willed them to continue.

'The number, it's burned onto my brain. J 4 NUS. Trouble was it wasn't registered to any one.' I spilled my tea in surprise. Matilda got up and got a cloth.

'Sorry' I muttered apologetically, covering my confusion. Another moments silence followed as we sat and drank tea, reflecting on the words that had been said. I broke the silence. 'Can I see a photo of her? Perhaps then if she is connected in any way it will trigger my memory.' Matilda nodded.

'Of course;' she stood up and walked out coming back with a photo in a frame. 'Her last school photo,' she said handing it to me. I stared at the young face smiling back at me through large round hazel eyes. It was a young version of the woman in my visions. The face was rounder, full of a youthful innocence and exuberance, her auburn hair long and curly. It looked as though she had attempted to tidy it for the photo but not quite got it right. I looked up to find them both watching me intently. 'Anything?' said Harry. I shook my head, it seemed best that way.

Harry stood and I knew my time was up. Standing, I shook hands with them both and thanked them for their time. Matilda watched as I drove out and I left feeling overwhelmed by emptiness.

Before driving home I stopped up by the shop and looked sadly at the road in front of me where I knew Rosie had been knocked down. I pulled out my note book and wrote down the information I had learned. I wrote the number plate in large letters:

J 4 NUS

Then underneath it: **J A NUS!**

Janus killed Rosie. It did not make sense but was that what I was meant to believe. Janus the mythological god that kept turning up everywhere I went. I drove home more confused.

Later that day after another awkward argument with Carna during dinner, I retreated to the study and sat once again reading through the growing notes, in the small notebook. I realised I had got as far as I could with Rosie and the children. I decided that if they were anywhere then they were in a parallel universe, for as far as this reality was concerned they did not exist and no evidence of them existed either.

That left the discovery of Geoff Price. He at least seemed to exist according to the girls in the office at work. So I felt sure if I could discover him I would get somewhere.

The following day after an abortive visit to his house where I discovered exactly what I had previously noted down. Geoff Price had lived there but moved over a year ago; to where the present owners did not know.

Carna was keeping out of my way now. We ate together and slept together but did little else. So I secreted myself back into the study and decided to find a private investigator. After a quick search on the internet I copied down the details of the nearest one, an ex-police officer who lived in the local town. A quick phone call followed in which we organised a meeting in a café that we both knew.

Getting in my car I wondered at what I was doing, feeling that the private investigator or P.I. was the exclusive preserve of the movies and television.

Arriving a bit later at the café, I stepped into its humid interior out of the rain. Realising a bit late that I had no idea what the man looked like, I wondered if we should have organised to both carry a certain newspaper or wear a certain flower or tie as they did in the films. My momentary uncertainty at the entrance was soon ended as an immaculately dressed ruddy faced gentleman stood and smiled at me. He was dressed in blazer and was wearing what looked like a regimental tie. I guessed that he was in his late sixties his hair was thin and what was there was carefully combed. I could not see his feet but I was certain that his would be wearing well-polished, well-worn brogues. I was not surprised to note his large tobacco stained moustache.

I walked towards him and he extended his hand.

'Reginald Palmer,' he said by way of introduction, 'you must be Francis.' I nodded, and looked round nervously, expecting everyone to be watching. Apart from a wan smile from a harassed looking mother trying to get her child to sit, the packed café seemed indifferent to my arrival. 'Coffee or tea?'

'Oh, tea please,' I said sitting.

'It's on me.' He said smiling as he headed to the counter. He soon returned with two mugs of steaming tea and a plate of biscuits. 'Couldn't resist,' he said putting them between us. 'Never can, I'm a dunker you see.' I looked at him now totally confused. His watery grey eyes sparkled at me. He picked up a biscuit and put it into his tea. 'Can't have a cup of tea without putting a biscuit in it,' he said by way of explanation. After a moment of dunking and slurping of tea, he continued, 'now to business;' wiping crumbs out of his moustache, 'you have a missing person you wish me to find.' I could not imagine him finding anyone.

'You do this often?' I said; he gave me a strange look. 'Finding people I mean.'

'What, oh yes, All the time; Well some of the time anyway. It's a sort of hobby, since I retired. Army and police you know.' He stared up at the roof and I guessed the old memories were flooding in. I coughed. 'Oh sorry where was I, yes that's it finding missing people. Most people ring me to find their lost dog or cat mind. Soon tell them they've got the wrong number. No, peoples the thing. Most of us detectives end up doing divorce cases, you know the sort of thing, watching the spouse, looking for infidelity. Can't say that's my cup of tea. Now *missing persons*, that's more like it.' He turned his grey watery eyes to me. 'So, what's the story?'

I wondered where to start and to be honest I wondered whether to start at all. I could not see much success in carrying on.

'Well, having doubts I see. Tell you what, no success no fee. How's that sound?' He dunked another biscuit. 'It'll certainly give me some incentive anyway.' After a moment's hesitation I agreed. Reginald pulled out a small battered spring bound notepad with a pencil stuck through its spring. He then produced some half glasses and perched them on his nose. He looked at me expectantly.

'So what's the background?' he prompted. I decided to tell him the barest details.

'I'm looking for a person called Geoffrey Price.' I explained that he had worked with me and gave him the old address, but told him that he had left there over a year ago.

'What's he look like? Got a picture?'

'Err, sorry no,' I looked in my notebook. At some point before my memory loss I had written a description, not much but I read it out. 'He's about my age, smaller, thinner. He was very thin then although that was over a year ago. Brown eyes, glasses, em…' I paused wondering how accurate this description was. Describing people accurately was not easy especially after a long time. I continued reading, 'mousy brown hair, bald patch at the back, freckles on his nose.' I dried up. That was it; not much to go on I thought. Reginald looked down at his notes.

'Should be enough to get going I should think. If you find a picture, that would help. Is he dangerous? I could not answer this as I did not know. I knew him before my memory loss. There were no notes to say that he was, in the note book, in fact what it said was more the opposite. I shook my head.

'No I don't think he's dangerous, he just has some information I ...' Reginald held up his hand to stop me.

'That's your business,' He interjected. 'I'll find him but I don't want to get involved in whatever's between you two.' He put his notebook, glasses and pencil away then gulped down the rest of his tea. 'Time I was off.' He said standing and picking up the last biscuit. 'Dog'll be needing a walk, been locked in the house all morning. I've got your mobile number I'll contact you when I've got something to tell you.'

'When...' once again he stopped me.

'You'll have to be patient. I'll go as fast as I can.' He smiled, 'must walk the dog first though.' His eyes glazed again at the thought of his dog and I guessed it was his main companion and friend. I knew what type it was before he told me. 'Called Scruff he is, fur in all directions, he's a terrier.' I nodded.

'Be hearing from you soon I hope.' We shook hands and he was gone. As I was readying to leave the waitress came over and handed me a bill.

'Did he not pay?' I said nodding towards the rapidly disappearing figure of my P.I. She shook her head and waited. I chuckled to myself and gave her some money. 'Keep the change.' This got a smile from her.

I headed out into the rain for my days adventures were not over just yet. I had another appointment with my counsellor who had some disturbing news.

I sat down in the chair by her desk and she looked me over. I tried to wipe the rainwater from my hair and face in an attempt to make myself look slightly more presentable.

'I see you've come alone.' She started. I realised that she had wanted me to bring Carna. I had forgotten in my rush to find evidence of my past. 'How have things gone Mr Smith since we last met?' She sat back and studied me. I explained that I had forgotten about bringing Carna. I do not think that went down too well. Then I filled her in on my attempts to discover my past, my visions of the family at the canal and playing football and of my visit to Rosie's parents and my hiring of a detective to find Geoff. She nodded as I spoke making notes. 'So Rosie did exist but she is dead, died when she was young.' I nodded. 'Did you bring your notebook?'

My hand reached up to my inside jacket pocket but I suddenly felt myself going defensive, not wanting to share this crucial bit of evidence, my lifeline, with someone who I felt was becoming more of a sceptic at each of my visits. I shook my head and mumbled an unconvincing, 'No.'

'Ok, I see.' She scribbled some more notes. There was a long silence while she made her notes. I studied the room. It was a small consulting room in my local surgery. Pretty bare, a couch, the chairs and the desk. There was one picture, a print, on the wall, not one to instil calm but one that expressed the tumult of feelings that went into being a human and having the luxury of thought. I recognised it as the Wave by the nineteenth century Japanese artist Katsushika Hosukai. The calm but powerful snow topped Mount Fuji in the background with in the forefront the Japanese fishermen fighting for the existence against nature's power of the great sea wave. I felt myself upon that rocking boat the sea spray washing over me, the taste of sea salt filled my mouth, the ocean scent my nostrils. The wave hung above me waiting for its supreme moment to engulf and overwhelm and yet it did not fall. Everything hung in the balance waiting...

'Huh hm.' She coughed to get my attention. 'Mr Smith.' I turned to her my eyes coming back into focus. 'I've been thinking that perhaps...' she would not catch my eye. I guessed my moment of judgement had come. She continued in a rush keen to get the words out and move on '...you may be suffering from a type of Psychosis and it may best for me to refer you on to a Psychiatrist, who may be best placed to help you.' She stopped and took a deep breath. I realised that she had had these words stored up since I had arrived and had been awaiting her moment to release them; The Wave.

'Psychosis,' I mumbled, 'A psychiatrist you say.' She nodded, finally looking me in the eye. She soon turned away when I replied, 'So you don't believe me? What I've been telling you in each meeting.'

'I am not able to judge, you just need someone more...' she looked at the ground. 'More experienced than me.'

'So that's it then.' I stood up. 'Might as well stop there I guess if I am going to have to tell it all to someone else. Mind I'm not sure if I want to. They will only form the same opinion as you. I guess on reflection my story is a bit hard to believe. I'm struggling with it myself.' She stood.

'You'll get an appointment in the post.' I nodded and left. I headed for my local pub feeling the desperate need for a drink and the sound of normality around me.

I pulled into the car park of the Coach and Horses and realised that I thought of it as my local but had no memory of going in and yet I must have done in the past. I stood before the entrance, feeling nervous, if it had been my local then those inside would know me. I pushed open the door. I was met by warmth and the gentle hum of the few occupants who liked to start their drinking early.

'Francis!' called the barmaid, raising herself from the elbows that she had rested on the bar. The two men who sat on bars stools supping their pints turned drinks in hand. 'It's lovely to see you. It's been a long time. I was beginning to wonder if you were still living round here. She moved up the bar away from the two men. 'Come and sit here and tell me what you've been up to. Still drinking the single malt?' She had the drink on the bar before I could reply.

'Err yes and thank you.' I replied passing her a five pound note. While she got my change I assessed this new bit of news. I had obviously been a regular. I took the change and sipped the drink.

'So...' she said leaning once again on the bar. 'What's the news? What has kept you from us for such a long time?'

'How long is it?' I enquired.

'Well let's see...' I watched her as she slowly tracked back through time. 'Christmas some time I reckon. No wait a minute you came in on your own for a bit on New Year's Eve.'

'Ah yes, I vaguely remember,' I pretended. 'Was I with anyone?' she shook her head

'No, you chatted to your neighbours, something about a hedge, if I remember right. Swallowed a few drinks and then left I think. It was some time ago now and it wasn't half busy that night. So what you been up to since then?' I debated to myself what I should say as I sipped at my drink. She watched me patiently, obviously glad of some different conversation.

'I had an accident.' I watched the surprise spread across her face. 'I collapsed, not sure why but lost my memory. I've been trying to work out what has happened since then.' She put her hand on mine affectionately.

'Oh that's terrible Francis. When was this?'

'Just after New Year.'

'I see. I have to say you did not look that good on New Year's Eve. I thought you had had too much to drink. Has it come back; your memory I mean?' I shook my head.

'I have flashes of memory but they seem to confuse me even more. It's as though I'm constantly chasing them and yet they are just out of reach. So...'

'Well what can I tell you?' I smiled at her and nodded encouragingly. 'Let's see. You used to come in here most weekends. Friday evening usually. Some times on your own sometimes with your lovely wife. Now what's her name?'

'R...' I stopped myself but her name had been there instantly. 'Carna,' I said tentatively.

'Yes that's it.'

'What did I used to chat about, and with who?'

'Oh you'd chat to the other locals and Paul the barman, usually about fishing and football. You know the usual man stuff.' I drank the rest of my drink, resigned to the fact that I would gain nothing new from the barmaid. Although I thought my neighbour might be worth a visit. The two other customers called her over for refills, which gave me the perfect excuse. I quickly finished my drink and waved at her as I headed for the door.

'Bye,' she called. 'Good luck, with...' she looked embarrassed not wanting to say anything in front of the two interested regulars. 'Well you know.' I nodded and thanked her. 'Don't leave it so long before you come back.'

I drove out of the car park, my agitation at the counsellor now slightly diffused with the effects of the whisky. I hoped there were no police in the area. I took it slow, driving the short distance back to the house. Instead of going in I decided to head round to the neighbours. Unsure which side to go I decided to head for the ones that always said 'hello' and seemed to be around every time I went out.

I parked the car on our drive and walked up the front path. Stepping on to the pavement, I looked back at the House. I noticed the large hedge that surrounded the property it was thick and luxuriant, covered in pink and white flowers. I recognised it as Hawthorn. It reminded me that sprigs of Hawthorn always filled a vase at the front door; they too were always covered in flowers. Two Ash trees stood like sentinels each side of the front path, between them the two doors beckoned the view made me shudder. On each side of the path were two perfectly manicured lawns in the centre of each, was a large Oak tree.

I had not studied the garden much since...; well, let's say I had no memory of plants in the garden. I realised I had not done any gardening and yet it all seemed immaculate. I guessed Carna must do it, though I had never seen her or anyone else working on it. I had a sense that there was more to the garden than I had realised, two doors, two ash trees, two oaks, the great hawthorn hedge down two sides, which I now realised had been in flower since my first memory. I decided to have a thorough look over it, front and back, when I had seen the neighbours.

I walked around to the small modern house next door and lifted my hand to knock but it opened.

'Hello Francis, come in, come in;' a small middle aged lady backed into the house beckoning me in with a smiling but intense expression. I stepped across the threshold.

'Err hello...' this was becoming my regular greeting for all the people I no longer remembered.

'Valerie,' she finished for me. 'It's ok; we had heard you had lost your memory after your collapse at the beginning of the year. Carna filled us in.' she turned and shouted surprisingly loudly for a small person. 'Peter, it's Francis from next door.' He appeared instantly from the back of the house as if he had been waiting for the call.

'Hello Francis;' he dashed forward and grabbed my hand giving it a hearty shake. 'Come in, come in,' he echoed his wife pulling me by my hand into the living room. 'So...' he said finally releasing me. 'Lovely to see you and what can we do for you?' he rubbed his hands together and leaned forward in anticipation.

'As you know I lost my memory a little while back after I collapsed at work.'

'Yes terrible thing. How are you now?'

'I'm ok but my memory well still not there I'm afraid.' Peter shook his head, an expression of sadness bursting from his face.

'Anything we can do to help?' his diminutive wife closed up beside him and mimicked his posture.

'What do you know of my past?'

'Come and sit down.' He turned to his wife, 'Tea, Valerie?'

'Yes dear. Francis?' I nodded and sat.

'Well, let's see now. You moved in next door just over a year ago.'

'Seventeen months,' Came a call from the kitchen. How she had heard us I do not know. She appeared at the door. 'You arrived on New Year's Day.'

'Yes that's right; a year before your accident. You did not have much to do with anyone really at the start. We first met you about this time last year, or was it a little later? Anyway we met you at the Coach and Horses. You got on well with the barmaid and some of the regulars. I think you went there regularly. I guess we did not speak to you often; just the odd chat when we bumped into you. That's about it I guess. Valerie?' She appeared carrying a tray with three mugs of tea.

'Yes that's about right. Not much else really. Your beautiful wife has never mixed much. She would always have a little chat about this and that if I saw her though.' She said passing out the mugs and sitting with Peter opposite me.

'New Year's Eve, I think I saw you then, didn't I?' I ventured, 'at the pub I mean. The barmaid said I had chatted to you when I was in there.' Peter smiled nervously.

'Err yes. We did see you then. You were on your own. Carna wasn't with you. '

'You did not look that well then.' Valerie added.

'It's probably not important but what did we talk about? Can you remember?' Peter nodded.

'I asked you about the hedge.' I looked at him confused. I could tell he did not want to elaborate. 'Asked if I could trim it a little;' he moved uncomfortably. 'It was a bit high at the front, you see; stopping the light, you know.' I did not because I had no memory of what it was like. But I had noticed it was squarely cut and ordered on this side and I realised high and wild on the other.

'Oh is that all?' he looked relieved and it had obviously been something that had concerned them. Confronting neighbours was never easy I decided.

I wandered back to the house musing on the fact that it had been a New Year's Day that I had arrived in the neighbourhood. This meant people had a memory of me here with Carna for a year.

She was not in the house so I wandered out into the garden. I noticed that the large hawthorn hedge continued down each side of the house and round the bottom. I could see the sloping green fields beyond it. The trees I realised were all oak and ash. Most of the garden was filled with grass with areas where it had been left to create meadow. The flower beds up around the house were filled with aromatic herbs, the scent of which filled the air. I breathed in deeply, my head awash with their perfume. The aches and stresses seemed to fade.

I heard a splash and turned to the pool house, pulling open the sliding door. Carna was swimming across the pool. She was naked and I felt the familiar stirring within me. She was irresistible. She turned and pulled herself from the pool. She knew I was watching. She turned slowly, seductively, throwing all her sexual arrows at me. For a moment my confused thoughts slipped my mind and I was happy to let them go to be replaced by this image of a naked goddess.

I found myself removing my clothing as I walked around the pool towards her. She stood waiting and watching; her arms outstretched. I was a marionette puppet and she pulled the strings. She pulled me down upon the large couch and the rest of the day disappeared in a drug like sexual haze. That night I slept better than I had in a long time, dreamless and deep.

It was not until the next morning after a large breakfast that memories of the previous day began to creep back. We were sitting at the kitchen table, the empty plates before us, coffee mugs in hand. It was difficult to get annoyed with her. She seemed so perfect, pliable and keen for me to be okay. She only ever baulked when I tried to question her, but I had to give it another go. I took a deep breath.

'Carna I have realised I don't know anything about my parents. I certainly haven't heard from them since my accident and I haven't come across any photos. I thought if I met them they might be able to jog my memory.' I looked at her expectantly. She pushed her long dark hair back over her shoulder and nodded, her high cheek bones causing her flawless skin to crease into a sad smile.

'I have not mentioned it because I did not want to upset you but I can see you now must know.' I nodded expectantly. 'You are an orphan.' I felt the breath escape me and my heart flutter. This was not what I expected and I shook my head.

'It cannot be.' I looked at her intensely.

'Well not totally an orphan I suppose but that's the way I...' she held my gaze 'and you always viewed it. You were put into care when you were a baby. You had problems in your foster home. They treated you badly and so you ended up in a children's home.'

I nodded. It explained the lack of photos. But somehow it felt wrong. It was the perfect inevitable explanation and I guessed if I researched it I would find it was all correct. I sighed.

My inability to accept this perceived reality grated. I felt enclosed, suffocated, as though I was fighting my way out of a giant bag – this universe – it just did not seem to fit; constantly at the back of my mind I now had a feeling that there was something else. I just could not fathom what it was.

The wonderful respite of the previous afternoon and evening seemed to evaporate. My coffee suddenly seemed tasteless. I wondered what would happen if I just left, but even at that thought I remembered the previous night. She had the ability to create such longing, I did not know if I could pull myself away from her. Besides if this really was my universe then I would be a fool to lose what I had.

My thoughts revolved in turmoil. I decided it was time to read Ovid so headed for the study via the lounge as I suddenly felt the need for an early drink to calm my nerves. With a whisky in my hand I retreated to the study closed the door and turned on the computer. While it powered up I read the notes I had made about Ovid and his writings plus the information that Carna's books seemed to be early manuscripts some of which were considered lost to the literary world.

I had to check for myself so quickly went back into the lounge. After listening for Carna and not hearing her I went over to her book shelf and was about to search through when I noticed the large black stone on the top.

I remembered that it was mentioned in the notebook. I placed my hand upon its smooth surface and suddenly found myself surrounded by light; I knew I should have felt scared but instead I felt calm. In the distance I could discern a robed figure watching me, a woman. I felt no threat just warmth and peace. The stone glowed beneath my hand. The moment I had released it I was back in the lounge. I shook my head, wondering what had just happened and collapsed into a nearby chair.

It was a moment before I realised why I had come in to the lounge. I determined to continue my search and trying not to look at the stone which now kept drawing my attention; I searched through the books on the shelves. Finding one entitled the *Fasti* and one called the *Medea* both of which I had mentioned in my notebook. The *Medea* should not exist. It had been lost to the modern world, yet here it was. I wished I could read the Latin script. I flicked through the *Fasti*. The notes had said that only six months were known and yet there was more than that here, I was certain. As I held the old text a thought struck me. These indeed did look old, the writing, the parchment, and yet they were in perfect condition, as though they had just been made, and yet I was certain that they were ancient and original not modern copies, besides who could copy texts that have been lost.

As I sat with them in my hands, they seemed to reach out to me. I had a vision of a man sitting on a stool in robes that could only be Roman, looking out across what Carna had described as the Macchia, Italian scrub, a large temple stood amongst it. It was no ruin; the plush newly sculptured marble shone in the bright sunshine. He bent down and with his quill began to write, scratching out the words on a piece of parchment which I knew was the one I was holding. I dropped the books, my heart pounding. The vision disappeared the moment the books left my hands. Picking them up, I looked guilty towards the door, I could hear Carna in the kitchen. Quickly I put them back on the shelf and went back to the study.

I rested my head in my hands, the two strange visions I had just had were racing through my head. Were such things normal, I could not believe so. Closing my eyes I concentrated on slowing my heart rate and refocusing. Eventually I pulled out the notebook and wrote down my experiences.

Sitting back in the chair contemplating I realised that I needed to look at the connection between Carna and Ovid. When I had recently searched for Carna, Ovid's name had been mentioned. I decided that this was the piece of Ovid literature that I needed to find. I followed the links of my previous search finding once again the script that I had copied down. *'Cardea was the ancient Roman Goddess of the Hinge. Roman doors being hung on pivot hinges. The Poet Ovid conflates her with another archaic goddess called CARNA whose festival was celebrated on the Kalends of June and for whom he gives the alternative name of Cranea, a nymph.'*

I suddenly remembered something that I had read in the notebook, something that I had written before my memory loss. I flicked back to the first page skimming down I found it, number 4. and read it again: *Who is Carna? Why did she appear different to me? Why will she not tell me what has happened? I am sure she knows. Why did she say you must know when to ask me?* It was the last part that had jogged my memory. 'You must know when to ask me.' I mumbled it again. 'Could that be the Kalends of June?' I mused to myself 'Whatever that is?' June was not far away now so if that was the time to ask her I needed to find out what it meant. With a rush of excitement I followed the link on the word Kalends. The word Kalendae in Latin meant 'the called' it was used to describe the first day of each month in the Roman calendar; the time when rest days would be announced for the coming month and when debtors had to pay up.

So would Carna tell all on the 1st June? It was mid-May so I did not have long to test that theory and test it I was determined to do. I went back to the page about Carna followed the link to Ovid. It led me on to an English version of Ovid's Fasti. I remembered from my previous notes that The Fasti was a book of the months of the year and that was why Carna's collection was special – it contained the missing months.

With my heart pounding, my mouth dry, I scrolled down to the month of June. Nothing could prepare me for the words I was about to read. The lines just tumbled through my confused mind.

Book VI –June 1st: Kalends

Carna, the first day is yours, Goddess of the hinge. She opens the closed, by her power, closes the open. The story of how she gained the powers she has, is obscured by time. But you'll still learn of it from my verse. There's an ancient grove of Alernus near the Tiber, and the priests still make sacrifices there. A nymph was born there (men of old called her Cranae); who was often sought in vain by many suitors. She used to hunt the land, chasing wild beasts with spears; stretching her woven nets in the hollow valleys. She'd no quiver, yet considered herself Apollo's sister. Nor need you, Apollo, have been ashamed of her. If any youth spoke words of love to her, she gave him this answer right away: 'There's too much light here, it's too shameful in the light. If you'll lead to a darker cave, I'll follow.' While he went in front, credulously, she no sooner reached the bushes than she hid: and was nowhere to be found. Janus saw her, and the sight raised his passion. He used soft words to the hard-hearted nymph. She told him to find a more private cave, followed him closely: then deserted her leader. Foolish child! For Janus can see what

116

happens behind him. You gain nothing; he looks back at
your hiding place. Nothing gained, as I said, you see!
He caught you, hidden behind a rock, clasped you, worked
his will, and then said: 'In return for our union, the hinges
belong to you. Have them as recompense for your
maidenhead.' So saying he gave her a thorn (it was white-
thorn) with which to drive away evil from the threshold...

I let out a sigh, and opened the notebook, my hands shaking I began to scratch down the words I had read. This allowed my tumultuous thoughts time to assimilate the words that Ovid had written so long ago.

Here was Carna and Janus both connected in Ovid's text. Carna born in the ancient grove of Alernus by the Tiber, I thought of the Sacred Isle that we had visited where Carna said she had come from, right by the Tiber. Carna raped by Janus and given the hinge, again I thought of the two large doors.

Then there was the white-thorn, it did not surprise me to discover after a quick search that this was Hawthorn – Crategus monogyna. This house was surrounded by it, a large vase filled with it stood between those two great doors. It was always in flower.

Somehow I knew that this ancient story was linked to this house, to my present reality. I determined to pin Carna down to some answers on the Kalends of June. I poured some more whisky into my glass swilled in round then gulped it down in one.

VIII

The next couple of weeks dragged by; I did not know how to pass the time. I could think of no further avenue of research. I had to wait for Reginald Palmer, P.I., to get back to me, and I was not sure that would ever happen, and I had to wait for the first of June.

I read more Ovid, slowly going through the known books. I discovered that on Carna's feast day that Mashed beans and lard was the meal, a type of refried beans, since this was the time of the bean harvest and beans had many magical-religious properties in ancient Rome.

The reading occupied my evenings along with copious bottles of whisky. It helped me to forget enough to find some rest at some point in the night. In the day I walked and fished, keeping my distance from as many people as I could. I did not think about work and nobody contacted me. My world was closed off, withdrawn. In fact, a rare hello from a passer-by would set me into a strange panic.

I kept away from Carna, She produced my food and sat and ate with me, but we did not speak. I did not go near the pool as it reminded me of our moments there. As it was, thoughts of her plagued my every waking moment. She had just accepted my need to withdraw and I think it partly suited her although she too looked sad and forlorn.

She seemed to appear at meals and disappear at other times. The house appeared ghost like but the moment I thought about her I would suddenly hear her moving about. She would pass the study door and smile in. My heart would be wrenched towards her. The air seemed to crackle with intensity. Then when she was gone the room would somehow feel different, filled with a dreaded emptiness which crept into my soul.

I found myself constantly thinking of the perfect moments when I was first recovering following my collapse. I had lived in a bubble, a dream in which all that I desired seemed to happen or appear. It all felt wonderful I had lived on a high for some weeks. Everything so real somehow but in a world in which I had no past. When I looked back it was the present with blurred edges. It could not possibly hold together unless I was prepared to forget myself, lose my identity and just live within the dream.

As I sat at my desk musing over the past six months I heard the letterbox go. I realised that we hardly ever received mail. I certainly had not seen any bills, or junk mail for that matter. I went out and picked up the letter.

It was an appointment to see a psychiatrist. I dropped the letter on the desk. I did not want to go. I already knew what they would say. I did not want to hide under a cloud of medication. I was not ready to accept it yet. If after everything, after I had investigated every possible strange pathway and found no way forward. When this life that I was now living seemed to be my only destiny then I would go.

The first of June arrived and I awoke with a sudden hope. But things did not go as I had been planning them in my head over and over for the last two weeks. My intention was to pin Carna down at breakfast before we went our separate ways and see if I could get some answers but on leaving the spare room I discovered that the house was quiet and empty. Even without going into the main bedroom I knew she was not there. The house echoed hollowly without her presence. There was a feeling of expectant waiting that filled the air as if the house itself was uncomfortable without her. Even the colours that filled every corner seemed dulled.

I pushed open the master bedroom door, feeling forlorn. Where was she? She was always around every morning filling the house with the smell of fresh coffee and the scent of breakfast.

The bed was made and cold. Always when I had thought about her she would miraculously appear and yet she was all that filled my mind this morning but nothing. I stood in the room at a loss, unsure what to do next; the scent of her lingered in the air. Agitated I quickly left the room and began to roam through the house, searching for her even though I knew I would not find her. I ventured into the pool house. Memories of her swimming naked through the water flooded my mind. I knew I wanted to see her there again even though I knew I would be sucked back in, that I did not have the self-control.

My anger grew. I ran into the garden and bellowed her name in anguish. It seemed to echo mockingly back at me off the large white blossomed hawthorn hedge that enclosed the garden. I ran into the house throwing things this way and that. Smashing everything in my path, systematically ransacking every room; my anger reaching levels I had never known before. I felt myself out of control. A wake of chaos, I crashed through the house, finally becoming exhausted I collapsed amongst my destructive mess.

Tears filled my eyes as I lay in the lounge amongst the torn remains of the Ovid manuscripts scattered around me like so much waste paper. I felt overwhelmed with guilt at the destructive force and anger that had raged through me. Now spent, I reached for the whisky bottle.

I sat amongst the mess for the rest of the day drinking whisky and sleeping, a pile of manuscripts for a pillow. It was late afternoon when I staggered out into the garden to vomit into the herb beds. Whilst kneeling and retching I felt a presence, even through the whisky haze. I raised my head and found Carna standing before me on the lawn. Her dazzling eyes penetrated my soul. My drunkenness dissipated. I rubbed my rough unshaven chin I felt dirty and unwashed before her. She seemed to glow, her long dark hair was piled up and full of whitethorn blossom. She wore a white shimmering toga that clung to her curves. She was a goddess and I felt unworthy.

'Where have you been?' I croaked. It was a whine, a plea and yet underneath my anger still bubbled. I felt ashamed before her.

'For weeks you have ignored me. You have used me. I have cooked for you been there every time you have thought of me; even slept with you every time you have wanted to. You have everything and I just wanted today.' I had bowed my head in shame as she spoke but at the last I grasped at her final word and stood up.

'Today yes, you would want today, your day, the Kalends of June, the feast of Carna.' I snarled angrily back. 'Today is the day you will speak? You will answer my questions?' My anger now turned to a desperate hope. She nodded.

'Come let us go in; don't be angry. Not today of all days. We can be at peace. I will answer …' I was about to speak but she held up her hand. 'But first I will prepare supper and you will wash and get yourself cleaned up.' It was a command that I found unable to disobey.

'The house…' I mumbled as she walked past me across the patio and into the back door.

'The house forgives you.' She said smiling over her shoulder.

I followed her in through the door, unsure of what she meant. I stopped stunned once inside. It was as if my morning's antics had not occurred. Every broken vase, ornament window, door and piece of furniture was as it had been when I had wandered the house early that morning looking for Carna. I picked up the nearest vase, a Romanesque pot on a side board by the door. It was filled with hawthorn blossom. I held the vase up studying it carefully. I could not see a single mark, crack or chip. In the black ornamented piece, the white temples and gods were as if they had just been painted and yet not minutes ago it had been shattered into hundreds of pieces with particularly brutal force. Its Romanesque connection had particularly riled me as I had headed for the garden. I wondered if it was an original piece and found myself laughing almost hysterically as I moved through into the immaculate lounge. My eyes were drawn to the bookcase, the Ovid manuscripts stacked in order, untouched and perfect. Even the bottle of whisky sat on the side full and unopened. Carna stood watching me silently. Then she came over and put her arms around me, hugging me close. I felt the soft warmth of her body and broke down. Tears flowed, soaking into the pristine whiteness of her toga. I lost track of time as we stood entwined but slowly calm seemed to seep into me. Her eyes too I noticed were moist. We kissed and I wondered if I was truly mad.

Finally she let me go. My frustration had turned to desire but she held me at arm's length.

'Supper' she said, 'whilst I prepare it you go and get cleaned up.' I realised suddenly that although the house was in perfect condition I was not. My clothes were dirty and I must have smelled pretty bad. I could not remember when I last washed. I went upstairs and stripped off. The shower soon washed away the dirt and allowed me to refocus my racing thoughts and emotions, which seemed to have touched every base in the last few hours. Remarkably my head seemed clear and I did not feel weary.

I remembered the plans I had for today and questions I was keen to ask. Flicking through my notebook, which was now constantly in my pocket, I wondered where to start.

Prepared and calm I returned downstairs and opened a bottle of Italian Red pouring it into two glasses. I carried them into the dining room where I could hear Carna moving around. We had not used this room as far as I could remember. It was a large room decorated with elegant antique furniture. A large dining table ran through the middle of the room above which hung a glistening chandelier. Food was laid out on the table and Carna sat waiting.

Giving her a glass I sat at the other end of the table, opposite her. Salad, fresh bread and a large dish of refried beans sat between us. I was suddenly reminded of some of Ovid's words and pulled out my note book. Flicking through quickly, I found the quote I had written down from the Kalends. I looked up at Carna; she smiled and waited patiently for me

'Yes here it is,' I found myself mumbling half to myself and half to Carna. Running my hand through my hair in agitation, I began to read.

'You ask why we eat greasy bacon-fat on the Kalends, and why we mix beans with parched grain?' I looked up at her. She nodded,

'Read on; he says things so well.' After a moment's hesitation I continued.

'She's an ancient goddess, nourished by familiar food, no epicure to seek out alien dainties. In ancient times the fish still swam unharmed, and the oysters were safe in their shells. Italy was unaware of Ionian heath-cocks, and the cranes that enjoy Pigmy blood: Only the feathers of the peacock pleased, and the nations didn't send us captive creatures. Pigs were prized: men feasted on slaughtered swine: The earth only yielded beans and hard grains. They say that whoever eats these two foods together at the Kalends, in the sixth month, will have sweet digestion.'

I looked up at her. She had a faraway look in her eye. After a moment she lifted her glass.

'To our sweet digestion.' I ignored her.

'Where have you been today?' It sounded abrupt but there was no room for small talk in my thoughts now. She smiled and took a sip of wine. She in turn ignored me.

'Tell me what you know of today; this special day.'

'The Kalends of June!' she smiled at my reply. I gulped down a large mouthful of wine then spooned some beans onto my plate. 'Beans, the symbolic festive food of the Kalends.' I passed them across to her. 'A festival in honour of Carna!' I raised my glass to her in a toast, a cynical smile on my face. 'I know what Ovid has told me!'

We ate silently for a while. As I chewed I deliberated what to ask.

'So today is the day,' I said finally; 'The day that you will answer;' she nodded.

'I can tell you some things, although there are still things you may need to discover for yourself.'

'So tell me what I need to know.'

'You must ask; I will answer.' After a moment's thought, I repeated the question I had previously asked.

'Where have you been today?' It was not the first question I had intended but for some reason I needed to know.'

'At this time each year I can return. Time has no measure. I go where people celebrate this day. Unfortunately that is in times gone by but I enjoy the release, the memories.' I did not know quite what to make of this; so contented myself with drinking some more of the Italian wine.

'You went to Ostia?' She smiled and nodded

'And the Sacred Isle?' She looked out of the window across the front lawn, lost in thought for a moment. I followed her gaze. 'But not as we saw it; as it was, vibrant, exciting, colourful, full of life and energy.' I tried to imagine those ruins covered in marble, the shouts and smells of a vibrant city. It would be a sight to see. I cleared the thought as I needed to focus if I was to find out what I needed.

'So you are Carna the Goddess?' she smiled and shook her head.

'Not a goddess, a nymph.'

'Which is?' Her smile reached into me, turning me inside out.

'My name at that time was Cranae. To be precise I am, or was, it has been so long I am no longer sure, a Naiad or freshwater or spring nymph. A Nymph is a divine spirit which animates nature. We appear as females to humans.'

'Beautiful females,' I mumbled my thoughts without thinking.

'Yes,' She muttered in reply.

'Ovid calls you goddess.' She nodded and stared out of the window.

'To him I was a goddess. He was one…' she seemed at a loss as to how to continue but I perceived her direction.

'One… you mean like me?' she nodded again. 'You liked him?'

'Yes, He was a good honest man, with much love in his heart.' She looked across the table at me, holding my gaze with her bright blue eyes. 'Much like you…Yes I liked him.'

We sat silently for a while and sipped at the wine. My mind grappled with the idea that this had been going on for so long. That she had been part of many lives, back to Ovid and before. Finally I continued.

'So you are immortal then. This has been happening for…'

'For many centuries, yes; I am immortal although I must live within this curse, laid upon me by Janus.' Her eyes glistened and a tear formed in the corner.

'Can it be so bad?' It came out before I thought what I was saying. I saw a flash of anger in her eyes. She stood up and turned away from me.

'To be so used! To watch men tear themselves apart as they are forced to face their lives turned upside down; made to see the other side. I am their perfection and yet I am their torment.'

'Every time, in every case I mean?' She turned back to me. Her anger gone, replaced by compassion. I felt her recognise me as one of those many men.

'Not always but mostly. You are here because you have followed a good life. You are a good man.'

'That's it! Just because I was a good man; I don't even know if that is true. There has to be more to it than that!'

'Well yes, good but striving, always looking for something more; believing that there is something better out there. At least that is how you were when you first came here, before you hit your head. You were also a man with a conscience; still are. There would have been no point in picking a weak or corrupt soul who would happily accept their new circumstances.' Comprehension dawned on me. I too, stood and walked up to her.

'So it is a test?' She took my hand and nodded.

'Sort of... Janus's joke on mortals... and me.' A sudden fear came over me as I had a vision of this powerful two faced god who could cause such suffering.

'Janus. Does he still exist? I mean like you, immortal.'

'In a way, yes. He is a true god after all.' She let out a short barking cynical laugh. 'Well he exists but not in body. His power is not so great as it was. Of the old ones there is only me that has physical form.' She gave a small smile of victory; 'and how that galls him!' I walked over to the window my head now swimming. I gulped at the wine from my glass trying as hard as I could to get my head around the idea that they existed, that myths and legends can be real. I heard her sit down behind me and went back to my seat. I knew I needed to stay focused and keep questioning.

'The Statue in Rome?' I said as I sat, reaching for the bottle of wine. We had drunk a lot but the bottle was still full. It no longer took me by surprise.

'Ah yes, he exists through such reminders; from which he tries to reach out and touch the living.' I passed her the bottle and she filled her glass.

'You shouted at it. In Latin I think. What did you say?'

She smiled and thought for a moment. 'It was Latin; I said 'Videte quid faciatis'. It means 'Look what you do.' I nodded sipping at my wine. 'Even a Naiad can become annoyed at times.'

'So what Ovid wrote in his book...?' I was unsure how to phrase my question. '...is that how it was? Is his story true? You know you and Janus?' I could see that this was a difficult question for her. Even after all this time there was pain there.

'Much of what he said is correct; for it was me that told him. He was ...' it was her turn to be stuck but I understood. She took a deep breath then continued. 'I told him the stories but of course he turned them into his Fasti.'

'You mean he didn't stick to your script. Embellished some bits left out others.' She smiled sitting silent for a moment studying her wine. I spooned up some bean stew. It was still warm. Carna's bowl was still full, untouched. 'Tell me about it.' She looked at me, confused. I clarified, 'You and Janus.'

'Ah, my story.' I nodded.

'It may help me to understand.' She smiled and my heart melted. She was truly stunning. She flooded my senses with one look and I momentarily forgot everything.

'I haven't told anyone since Publius.' It was my turn to look confused. This time she clarified. 'Ovid.'

'Oh yes, Publius Ovidus Naso, sorry forgot; had quite a lot to take in recently.'

'Few have been interested in my story and I have told even less. Why should I tell you?' I was not sure how to respond.

'Because I am interested in you; you are part of my puzzle.' Again she smiled. I quickly looked away not wanting to get distracted. 'And perhaps because I have asked and you have said you would answer on this day.'

'True, true; I will answer you. Not for the reason that it is the Kalends but because I truly like you and feel that although you are lost and wanting to find your past you do not hate me for being here. I will for the fact that you are interested in me; for few men have been.' With her looks I found that hard to believe. She seemed to read my thoughts. 'Looks aren't everything when you are stuck in a nightmare and have not the ability to rationalise and find what you need to reshape your life. Many have come to hate me for the fact that I reflect the perfection that they have always dreamed of. Others of course have just been happy to use me.' She paused. 'So where would you like me to start.'

'The beginning is as good a place as any.' She chuckled.

'My birth then, I guess.' She took a deep breath, I settled back in my chair clutching my glass tight in expectation. 'I was born on the Sacred Isle, the place we visited. I nodded in understanding. 'My mother was Cybele.' She waited, I racked my brains and then it came to me.

'The mother goddess!' I almost shouted, 'We visited her temple in Ostia... Your mother!' she nodded glad that I had remembered. 'Your father...?'

'My father was Alernus, a river god, Ancient even then. I knew him little and saw him less. My mother did not speak of him much. I was named Cranae then, as I mentioned earlier. I lived amongst my fathers sacred groves upon the island. I was a nymph, mortal but long lived, protected from the afflictions that affect and take away human lives. My special talent, and perhaps my curse, was to always appear the picture of female perfection in a man's eye.

As a child I roamed happily in, what was then, a wild land called Alerrius. I became a renowned huntress but also the hunted, for, as word of my looks spread men began to seek me out. At first, when I was still young and innocent, I found this flattering and fun. I would play with their emotions then leave them floundering. Often I would lose them in the woods and scrub land which I had come to know so well. My mother had left me in the care of an old woman in the woods. Her name was Claudia; yes Claudia Quinta.

Claudia was old then but much loved by my mother for it was she that had helped bring my mother- Cybele's image to Rome along the Tiber.

When my mother's image arrived in 204 BC the waters of the Tiber were drought ridden and unyielding to the arrival of the ship...' I held up my hand interrupting her.

'What do you mean by your mother's image?'

'Patience, let me finish, then you will understand. As I was saying there was a drought and the boat was stuck fast. Claudia called upon my mother. Claudia had been much maligned, none believed her chaste and rumours abounded about her. I will use the words that Publius gave her after I had told him the story for he was poetic *'Kind and fruitful Mother of the Gods, accept a suppliant's prayers on this one condition: They deny I'm chaste: let me be guilty if you condemn me. Convicted by a goddess I'll pay for it with my life. But if I'm free of guilt, grant a pledge of my innocence by your action: and, chaste, give way to my chaste hands. "She spoke: then gave a slight pull at the rope. The goddess stirred, followed, and, following, approved her. Witness the sound of jubilation carried to the stars...* He goes on but suffice to say the boat moved up the river!'

'Sorry' I butted in, annoyed with myself for breaking her flow again but needing to understand. Your mother arrived on a boat, your goddess mother. I'm still a little confused.'

'Her image, I said, remember. The Romans had gone to Greece, to Pessinus where my mother, Cybele's power and presence rested within a large Black Stone. It is this they brought back to Rome and placed in the temple there. In Rome they called her the Magna Mater, the Great Mother.'

'The black stone in the other room...!' I exclaimed.

'Yes, the very same. It came from the stars, from the gods themselves.' She smiled.

'A meteorite?' she nodded

'Yes that is what you would call it.'

'Is your mother still within it?'

'A part of her, why?'

'I felt it. Or I felt something...'

'When you put your hands upon it?' I nodded.

'It was calming, warm, it was as though...' I shook my head unsure remembering the feeling.

'As though you were part of all things.'

'Yes...' I muttered feeling somewhat awestruck at the thought. For a moment we were silent; both sipping quietly from our glasses of wine. I soon felt the need for more information.

'In those days she was not just in the stone. She can't have been for you to exist.'

'As I explained with Janus. Then she was worshipped by many. This gave her power enough to exist outside of the images that are connected to her. The power of the Gods is dependent on their followers.' I nodded my brow furrowed with concentration as I tried to take it all in and comprehend this 'other' world.

'Shall I continue?' I looked up she was watching me intently a wry smile on her face.

'Oh yes, sorry.'

'Back to Claudia Quinta then; she dedicated herself to my mother and also to me when I came upon the scene. She was good to me and I came to love her as much as she loved me. She taught me herbs and gave me earth knowledge but I grew up a wild temptress. She warned me to be careful, but.... Well the tempestuousness of youth. Though in my defence, I did not ask for those men to come. I was as happy without them; wearing skins, I would chase deer with my spear through the Maccia. Now looking back it was such a short time in my long life and yet it was so...'

'Precious,' I finished for her. She nodded.

'Yes, childhood is so important in our development and so precious to our memories.'

'I cannot remember.' I said solemnly.

'Mm. I am sorry for that; it is not good to not remember your youth, your roots.' She fell silent, her expression full of sadness for herself and the passing of her innocent exuberant youth and for the lack of knowledge that I now had of mine.

'You know,' I said, 'you remind me of a character I have recently read about in one of the books in the lounge-Don Quixote by Cervantes. I suppose as the book is on the shelf in there I am guessing it has something to do with you. I cannot remember the character's name; let me think.'

'Ah yes. Marcela, the shepherdess.' Her eyes became distant. *'I neither love nor hate anyone; I do not deceive this one or court that, or trifle with one or play with another.* Poor Chrysostom he would not listen. He believed his love should be returned just because Marcela was beautiful and he had declared his love for her. The poor deluded man died when his love was rejected.' She looked out of the window. 'He was another one, like you, Miguel I mean. Sorry Miguel de Cervantes Saavedra.' She turned and smiled

'You knew him then. Of course you did! That book was old, sixteenth century I think. So even that story came from you. Marcela, in his story that was you wasn't it?' She nodded. 'He was telling your story.'

'In his own way and fitted to his own time; Yes, Like Publius, sorry Ovid, had done earlier. I liked him; Cervantes I mean; another good man, although troubled. I like to think I helped him to see through the shallowness of the society that existed around him.'

I found it strange to think of her with so many different men over thousands of years.

'Did you drive any to death? Was he telling a real tale?' it took her a moment to reply.

'There was one. The tale that Miguel recounted; it was the beginning of my troubles, when I was young and still living wild in the Maccia, like Marcela. The man that Cervantes called, Chrysostom; He followed me around, would not leave me alone. I kept sneaking away from him. It was fun at first but he would not give up. Anyway to cut a long story short, he eventually took his own life.' She was calm, but I could hear the emotion in her voice and feel it in the atmosphere.

'Have there been others, you know like me, since Janus that have not made it?' I was not sure I wanted an answer to this question.

'After, well you have felt the pain and emotion; Some good but weaker men have not coped, but I do not see it as my fault as I did not with that first man.

It is the circumstances that they have found themselves in. They have not been able to find a pathway through. I like to think I have not caused any death; in fact, I do my best to make it easy within the boundaries set by Janus.'

'Why don't you stop?'

'If I stop I die. Besides I cannot even if I wanted to. It is Janus' curse.' She barked a cynical laugh which made me jump. 'Don't get me wrong it is not all that bad. I get to experience the ever changing world. I effect change through the men I meet. Many like you are worthy companions.

And at least I get to live in human form. He does not and he so wants to. I feel him all the time. Like the rest of them, all gone, trapped now in the ruins of their temples and monuments unable to do or affect anything.

It hurts them. I do not mind that it hurts him but Cybele… my mother I feel her she watches the pain that humans cause on the earth. I feel her tears.' She too began to cry. It caught me by surprise. I found myself round by her side holding her. I had no memory of moving.

'Sorry. It's just I feel it through her.' I thought, how strange it was that after all this time, the fact that she was immortal, she was not human but a semi-goddess, that she still had so much emotion, human emotion at that.

'Back to your story?' I suggested. She nodded wiping her eyes.

'Go, sit down, I'm alright. I will continue.' I did as I was told.

'Janus... so what happened? Did he really have two faces?' I said as I collapsed back down in my seat. An image of the roman statue filled my thoughts.

'No but he could see all things. There was no hiding from him. Of course I did not know that at the time. Anyway some of the men that had come chasing me had gone to the Janus temple and called upon him. He heard their story of love lost, of the man who had died.

They wanted vengeance because of course, it was all my fault!' she said with angry sarcasm. 'Men! They can understand so little. I would have been quite happy just to be left alone. Anyway it piqued his interest and he came looking for me. He found me in the Sacred Grove. I tried to escape but... well you cannot hide from Janus.' Tears began to fall once again down her face. I rose but she beckoned me to sit. 'I have been treated badly many times since but then I was innocent. I just wanted to be myself. He pinned me down and took me.' She finished and gulped at her wine.

'Raped you!' I found the anger rising within me. She nodded.

'But that was not the end. The gods are often cruel. It is why I pity few of them their fate. Although, I think he felt some guilt. I like to think that he realised that he had become no better than the men that had come to him. I think he blamed them for his lapse. He wanted to challenge those men that professed to be so honest, innocent and righteous, when he saw my pain. So it was that he tied me into challenging such men for all eternity. It helped to assuage his guilt.'

'I would not want…'

'I know but time changes the challenges we face. You were one who truly believed that your direction was the only way. You were blinkered; you were judgemental; quick to form opinions unable to perceive the situation from another's perspective. You were content, but your wife… it is easy to expect, to take for granted. It is why you are here.' I shook my head unsure, as I could not remember; in my visions all had seemed well, but I guess they had been images from my memory. I could not agree or disagree. I had just assumed that everything had been perfect in my past life but I suddenly realised that it might not have been so.

'There must have been worse than me.'

'Oh yes there are plenty worse. This is not about best or worst, just human nature but in the end it comes down to fate. You were there when Geoff needed someone and you fitted. '

'Why…? How …?'

'I cannot tell you. You are looking for him. If you decide to find him, ask him.'

I gulped at my wine unsure now. I had not even been sure that Geoff had really existed. My mind was flooded with wine and by what I had heard. I felt I should not believe it, but after everything that had happened I knew it was true.

'So …' I finally said. 'My world, my old world, Rosie, my err…wife, my children, Theresa and Michael did they exist.' I moved uncomfortably. 'Do they exist?' I added before she could answer. Her piercing eyes glistened as she watched me. It all seemed other worldly.

'This is why you are here, because even when you are offered everything you could desire you do not let go. You hold on to what you left behind.' I could not look at her for even though I searched for my past I knew I desired her and if the time ever came I realised I would find it just as hard to leave her. I screwed my eyes shut trying hard to focus on the family I had seen in my visions.

'Do they exist?' I repeated.

'That depends on you Francis. Janus gives you two possibilities. The first is that you accept this new life and what was, never was or the second is that you give this up.' She waved her hand around her indicating the house and herself.

'And return?' I still refused to look at her.

'Janus does not let you off so easily. It is not his way, but it is possible to return.'

'How?'

'You are on the path. It is for you to find the way and face the challenge that such a choice will give you. I cannot direct you more on this. But I want you to know I will support you and am here for you whichever choice you make.

Is there anything more that you wish to know from me, for the day is drawing to a close?'

I looked down at my watch. It was not the watch I had been wearing that morning but one I had seen advertised recently and admired, Swiss and expensive.

'Did Geoff get to return?' she nodded assent. 'Will you tell me how?' she shook her head.

'No, as I said, that is your challenge.'

I sat back feeling the wine flushing through me making it hard to think.

'I think I am drunk for the second time today!' I blurted.

'Do you want to be?' I shook my head, my vision going blurry. Suddenly my head cleared. I felt as fresh as when I had woken. I stared at her.

'Thank you.'

'You need to think clearly. It is your one chance; unless of course you wait until next year!'

I pulled out my notebook and skimmed through the pages looking for unanswered questions.

'My memory will it return?'

'That was not directly caused by... by your situation. Well it was but... Oh how can I explain?' She thought for a moment 'You collapsed because of the stress you were under. Your memory loss was due to this. You could not cope with remembering. You shut it out. So it could come back. That is up to you.'

'So those in the past did not suffer memory loss?'

'It has happened but most...No.'

'But I thought with your brew?'

'Ah that. Well it helps relaxation. It helps the mind to find a different path. That can involve shutting out the past but that depends on the person. It stopped your visions.'

'Yes my visions. They were my past weren't they?'

'Yes'

'They made me feel as though that was where I should be. The notebook...' I fingered it. 'It challenges me not to forget.' I was suddenly full of doubt. 'But how can I be sure. If I don't remember everything how will I know that I should return or stay here?'

'I cannot help you. This is your decision. It is how Janus works. To create a dilemma; two possible solutions, each could be plausible to you. You no longer have that certainty that you know the way. That your path is the only one.'

'If I stay, I stay here with you.'

'Yes, here you have what you desire, although it is not forever. There is a time limit.'

'Then what; what do you mean? Carna stood and walked across to the window again. The curtains were open. In the sudden silence the wind could be heard rustling the trees outside, a few spots of rain had dashed the window.

'Not nice weather for June.' She murmured. She turned and looked back at me running her hands through her long black hair. She looked tired. That surprised me, but then a lot had happened over the last twelve hours. 'You get nineteen years to the day.' Again I felt confused. Even if I stayed it would not be for life.

'I don't understand. If I stayed just when I was settled in this life it would all change again. Why?'

'After nineteen years… two hundred and thirty five lunar months, the sun and the moon will be in the same position as they were when you came here.' She barked another cynical laugh. 'Janus will then throw you back. It is the price of staying'

'Back…? You mean I would automatically return to that other life?' She nodded her head without looking at me. 'Will they be there then my family?'

'Yes, but they will be nineteen years older like you. You will be the missing father returned.'

'I will miss their youth.' I muttered, wondering why I was concerned as I did not really know them; 'If I find a way to return before that?'

'The clock gets set back to the moment you came here.'

'I have been driven to finding my past.'

'I know' she walked over and put her arm on my shoulder. I felt her presence, her warmth close to me.

I think it was a good life…' I looked up at her for reassurance.

'It was for a human relationship. It could have been better and will be if you return and learn from your experience.'

'Learn?'

'It may seem strange but it is what Janus wants. Learn to value what you have, to value others and their opinions; to give others time and not be so self-driven; to give and not just receive; to love freely, without expectation.'

I leant on the table and put my head in my hands. I was at a loss. Now I had been given the choice. Now I knew what had happened to me I no longer knew what I wanted. I realised that although there was a choice I did not know at present how I was to return if that was what I decided.

'I don't know what I am meant to do!' I said despairingly. She knelt beside me. I felt her breath upon me. It was like a dawn breeze, calming me. She took my face in her hands and kissed my forehead.

'You have learnt much tonight. The day is all but done. Come let us go to bed. Sleep and be refreshed so that you can think clearly tomorrow.' She took my hand and I blindly stood, glad to be lead, without having to think. In the hall the grandfather clocks hands came together at twelve midnight and the mechanism began to whir, preparing to chime. I stopped woken from my thoughtlessness for one last moment as I stared at the two doors. Carna turned at my abrupt halt and looked at me enquiring.

'The clock has not yet chimed.' I said quickly. 'The doors, why are there two doors. I cannot open that one. The notebook says that they were here when I first came. They were on Geoff's house.' The clock began to strike. Carna smiled and squeezed my hand.

'You are persistent, and you have great powers to resist. The doors, yes, they are on each and every house I live in. they are a gift from Janus....' She studied them as the clock hit its sixth chime. 'The beginning and the end,' She turned to me 'they are your way in and your way out.'

'Enigmatic' I said quickly 'explain...' the clock had hit its twelfth chime. She shook her head.

'We are done. Midnight has come and gone. You must find the way.' She turned back and began to walk up the stairs 'or wait until next year and ask me then.' She reached out her hand to me. I took it. Once again lost in her spell and she led me up the stairs.

IX

I woke late the next morning to the smell of coffee and baking. It had been almost light when we had finally fallen into an exhausted sleep. Pulling the covers off I decided on a quick swim before heading for the inviting smells of the kitchen.

It was refreshing in the cool waters of the pool. The sun shone through the large windows, a contrast to the wind and rain that had got up as the night had gone on. As I swam slowly up and down I began to re-run over the events of the previous day. I knew I needed to write things down quickly before I forgot and determined to do so as soon as I had breakfasted.

The thought of Carna's breakfast and the urgency of the need to focus and go through the previous evenings events meant that I curtailed my swim and headed into the house. Carna was waiting there. She watched my arrival with a certain nervousness it seemed, unsure of how our relationship should progress after the previous day's discussions. I mused that our night's activities should surely have settled her somewhat. I knew my feelings for her had grown and become undoubtedly deep, which made my thoughts on what I should do even more troubling.

I took her hand and kissed her, her presence once again sucked away my anxiety. We sat and ate fresh drop scones and drank smooth fresh coffee. We spoke little until we had finished. Then with a slight cough to draw my attention, Carna said,

'I realise you have a lot to get your head round. I know it will not be easy for you. As I said last night, I will be there for you. When you need me you only have to think or call out. I will hear you.' She smiled coyly and reached across holding my hand on the table. You are a special man and I am happy to be with you.' A dark thought flashed through my mind.

'Do you say that to all of them?' I had gone to pull my hand away but she held on. She shook her head.

'No! Very few; some you know. I have had occasion to judge every kind of man in the last few thousand years and very few have I felt any sense of attachment to.' She held my gaze, boring into my soul.

'Ovid, Cervantes...?' she nodded

'And you!'

'Any others that I would know?' I still felt agitated, although the longer I held her gaze the more I softened.

'Some may be but it is of no matter. Focus on now and try not to get too bogged down with my past.'

'Yes, I have enough trouble with my own!' I grunted sarcastically; 'and my future to for that matter!'

'You do.' She murmured in agreement and squeezed my hand. I so wanted to be angry with her but was just unable to be. She had absorbed all my negative emotion. Standing I grabbed a coffee refill and headed for the study.

Sitting at the desk I pulled out my notebook. I wrote down the key points of Carna's story from the previous night plus the answers she had supplied during my questioning.

When I had finished I sat back, the book in my hands and gave a big sigh. I seemed to have discovered much that I had so wanted to know such a short time ago. I seemed to have found answers to virtually every question that was in the notebook, although one of the first entries into this now rather battered notebook still stumped me. It was entry number two. I read it slowly as I leaned back in my comfortable leather desk chair. '2. *Everything had changed when I arrived with Geoff at his house. Note-need to find Geoff.'* Need to find Geoff. Was this the key to the one puzzle left; how to return.

I got up and began to pace the room, for doubt flooded my thoughts. I no longer knew if that was what I actually wanted. How could I be? I had no memory of that other world. In many ways it was more alien now than where I was, especially as now I understood how I came to be here. I had gained a history of sorts, my confusion had moved from needing to know, to tracking down my past, to now trying to decide which existence I actually wanted.

I felt exasperated; being given the choice of two lives, one that was and one that is. If I choose the one that is, it lasts just nineteen years then I will find myself back in a world that I will have even less comprehension of.

That evening instead of retiring to the study and keeping out of Carna's way I joined her in the lounge. She handed me a large crystal tumbler of tawny Islay whisky. I span it slowly as I sat and watched her. It was a warm evening. I had sat little in this room recently, too agitated and not wanting to face Carna. It had been her den, her space, mine had become the study. Now though, after the previous evening, things felt subtly different.

She sat curled up on the sofa, a book in one hand a glass of wine in the other. She looked up and smiled at me. She evoked a feeling of warmth and comfort. There was, and never had been I realised, any feeling of pressure or expectation from her. She did not ask for anything just accepted. I sighed and sipped at my whisky. I felt more relaxed than I had in many days.

I noticed a pile of new books on the coffee table that was between us. So put my drink down and picked up the top copy, chuckling as I read the title. I felt her eyes on me. I sat back and began to read.

'*The First Book of the Metamorphoses of Publius Ovidius Naso. From bodies various form'd mutative shapes, my muse would sing: - Celestial powers give aid! From you those changes sprung, -inspire my pen.*'

I felt her eyes upon me and looked up.

'I have only read four lines and I sense you in this already.' She looked away awkwardly.

'I guided him. He was...'

'A bit of a lothario from what I have read, Lots of lovers, lots of erotic poetry.'

'You must remember that times were different and such things were viewed differently. The emperor Augustus had only just made laws regarding monogamous marriage. It was not something that Publius could agree with. He was an idealistic poetical politician and that did not sit well with the authority. He became the lover of Julia the Younger, the emperor's daughter and got mixed up in a conspiracy against Augustus. At that time I was with a roman legate by the name of Valerius. He knew of Ovid and did not want to see him put to death.

He passed me over to Publius.' She paused I could see she was not comfortable with this last piece of information so did not push her to explain. I just assumed it had something to do with two large doors.

'Anyway to cut a long story short, through my connections with gens Fabia I was able to save him and we went into exile to Tomis. It was there he wrote what you are reading and the Fasti.'

This time I did need some explanation.

'gens Fabia?' I looked at her questioningly.

'Yes. They were the most ancient patrician family in Rome. Their history was full of leaders, warriors and the like. I had had many connections with them in the past and was seen as part of their family.'

'What does it mean gens Fabia?'

'Oh the family of Fabia.' She chuckled 'Fabia comes from Faba which means bean.'

'Bean…! You…!' I stammered 'the Kalends feast!'

'As I said I had many dealings with the family. The histories say they go back to Romulus who was known as Quinctilli and Remus who was known as Fabii.'

'And you would know whether the historians were right!' she laughed. It was a strange conversation but I found myself enjoying this voyage of discovery.

'Tomis; didn't we visit…' she held her hand up to stop me.

'No, you're thinking of Sulmona or Sulmo as it was in 43BC. That was where he was born. We went there on our Rome trip. Tomis is in what is now Romania. It is now called Constanta. It is on the Black Sea coast.' I nodded

'Was it part of the Empire then?'

'Yes, but only recently captured. Publius wasn't happy there; but at least he was alive. He called it 'a war stricken cultural wasteland on the remotest margins of the Empire.' He wanted to be back in the political heart of things, but… well I worked on him. You can be happy anywhere if you want to and you have all the basic essentials and we had more than enough there. I turned him to his writing and assisting the poor people of that land for they had been badly bruised by the Roman invasion and they were only slowly recovering.' She got up and walked over to the bookcase coming back with one of her ancient books. 'Here take this. It is the original

146

manuscript of Metamorphoses. He wrote it in Tomis. Read some words. You have felt it before.' I could not hold her gaze, remembering the time I had come in and sat looking through these books. 'You have seen him.' I reddened slightly.

'So he wrote these?' she nodded. I looked down at the first page and began mumbling the Latin words, not understanding.

Suddenly I found myself standing in a villa on a mosaic floor of a god crowned and proud sitting, holding a staff. It was full of colour and glory. Hearing a noise I looked up to see a man sitting on a veranda at a low table. His face was creased and tanned from too much sun. He had a smattering of hair around the sides and a balding pate to his head. His most striking feature was his large nose.

I moved forwards nervously. A woman stood next to him. They looked out across a wild dark green scrub land which ran down to a long curving beach, a glistening sea lapped gently at the white sand. To one side a small community of cottages, shacks and houses some stone but most wooden surrounded by a balustrade butted up against the shore where numerous sailing craft lay pulled up. Smoke rose up from cooking fires in the still air. Amongst the houses I could see a new marble temple in the roman style. I noticed roman soldiers at the nearest town gate.

The woman began to speak. I had moved forward and stood not far from her now. She was speaking to the man. I could not understand their conversation. She squeezed his shoulder as she stood over him. He smiled up at her and picked up his quill pen, dipped it in some ink and began to write. I moved closer, I felt as though I was dreaming. I could see the Latin words appearing the ink fresh upon the parchment, glistening in the bright sunlight as it dried. I recognised the page; it was the one that I had been holding. Suddenly the woman looked at me and smiled. I stepped back in shock. She was older her hair greying, her face rounded, but the eyes I recognised. She spoke again to the man who grunted and carried on with his work and then beckoned to me to follow her. She walked into the house across the mosaic floor and through an archway. Following her I found myself before two great bronze doors. I knew them instantly.

I turned back to the woman but found myself staring at Carna. I was back sitting on the sofa, holding the book. I felt faint.

'It was him, wasn't it?' She smiled; 'He was writing those words; the ones that I just read.' I quickly picked up the English version. '*The First Book of the Metamorphoses of Publius Ovidius Naso.*

From bodies various form'd mutative shapes...

You were there too. Weren't you? It was you, wasn't it? Different, but those eyes, your eyes...' I was mumbling now. She poured me another whiskey and gave it to me. I drank it down all in one feeling the fire of the liquid course through me. I coughed and spluttered but felt revived. 'Thank you. Sorry but that was a bit intense. Even after everything I have been through over the last few days!'

'Yes it was me.' She said sitting next to me on the sofa and placing her hand on my leg.

'It was strange seeing you, and yet seeing someone else.' I took a sip of whisky. My heart beat had slowed. 'That mosaic, beautiful but who...?' She chuckled.

'One of Publius's jokes; Jupiter King of the gods. He liked the idea of stepping on him every day.'

'Didn't Jupiter object?'

'Their power was waning. It was the time of emperors. Temples were still being built but the gods weren't expected to leave them anymore.'

'Ovid wasn't one who was much in love with the gods then?'

'No if you finish Metamorphoses, you will see how much. He tries to invert the accepted order, elevating humans and their passions and at the same time ridiculing the gods and humourising their passions and conquests.' I had gingerly put down the manuscript not wanting to find myself suddenly back in time and picked up the English copy.

'I'll give it a go, shouldn't take me too long.' I said feeling the weight of the smallish book.

'That is book one. There are fifteen books to Metamorphoses.' She said pointing at the table.'

'Ah, might take a while, especially as it is written in poetry.'

The following day as I stood on the bank of the lake lazily casting my line into the glistening water, mulling over my view of the Black Sea two thousand years ago, I wondered whether in fact I should just sit back and try to live and enjoy this, especially as at present it seemed the only path open to me.

By the end of that day as we headed to bed I found my will to keep searching for change failing me. Watching Carna undress my thoughts were filling with the benefits of remaining where I was.

And as the days progressed I soon slipped into an easy pattern, getting up swimming, breakfast, walking or fishing, shopping; Carna forever at my side. I did not think of returning to work. Carna did not mention it and work never contacted me. It just seemed unimportant. When I tried to talk finance with Carna she just replied with: 'There will always be enough if that is the way you want it.' I stopped questioning and just soaked up the luxury of the situation I now found myself in. As I had done before I shut out any thoughts of my past. I had put the now rather full notebook in the study desk drawer.

It was not until August during a holiday touring Spain that I once again found myself facing our pasts. Spain was Carna's choice and I had wondered if there was a reason behind it but she had refused to say anything.

We were nearing the end of our tour. We had been along the coast and were now on our way to Madrid to fly home. Our last stop before Madrid was Toledo.

We approached Toledo in the late afternoon across what Carna informed me was La Mancha. That name sounded familiar but I could not place it. She told me that it was a large windswept plateau which explained the fascinating groups of white circular windmills with their conical, hat like, roofs. We travelled past vineyards, olive groves and fields of sunflowers, finally crossing the Tajo River that ran through a gorge around the edge of the city. It sat upon a rise dominated by its cathedral and a castle called Alcazar. I could see no apartment blocks towering upwards which was a pleasant surprise. Carna had become more animated the closer we got. I knew she had been to Spain and seemed to have known many of the places we had visited but she seemed different. I realised she was reminding me of the time we had gone to Rome. There was a connection here that was important to her. My interest was piqued. I did not press her as I knew I would find out soon enough.

We drove into the old town's centre and found a small hotel that had a room. I was no longer surprised by the fact that everywhere we wanted to stay they always seemed to have one room left even at the height of the season. I knew that it was Carna's magic as I was beginning to call it.

That evening we picked out a small cosy restaurant in an old back street recommended by the hotel owner. It oozed atmosphere. I sipped at a reasonable Spanish wine, the air from a whirring overhead fan just about kept us cool. Across the table Carna looked as radiant as ever.

'This is a beautiful town.' I leaned back enjoying the gentle sound of Spanish guitar in the background. I watched her carefully to see what reaction I would get and said 'you seemed more animated than usual at our arrival here.' I noted surprise and continued. 'You have been here before and...' she was holding her breathe, '... you have good memories of this place.'

'You have come to know me well in a short time Francis. My memories of our time will always be good ones.'

'What of those you have of this place?' I said not letting her deflect my enquiries.

'Ah well, are you sure you want to know? We haven't talked much about such things for a while.'

'Since the beginning of June,' I said smiling. Perhaps it was the atmosphere or the wine but I found myself wanting to delve back into her fascinating past. 'Tell me.'

'Okay if you're sure...' I could see she was not keen but nodded at her and smiled encouragingly. She took a deep breath

'I was here in 1583...' she watched me allowing my brain to absorb this fact and analyse what it meant. Finally I got there.

'Of course! I knew I had come across the name La Mancha before. It just didn't register when you mentioned it as we drove in. Don Quixote de la Mancha, the hero of Cervantes' book. You were here with him weren't you? Cervantes I mean.'

'Yes, Miguel had just returned from the Azores where he had been part of the King Philip's army; they were trying to conquer Portugal. Miguel had left his regiment and was passing this way as he returned to his home town of Alcala de Henares which is not far from here. He was at a loss. He had little money and no direction. He had a heart of gold. And so it was that he was brought to me. We lived here in Toledo for some years but he wanted to return... you know go back to his past. He was a restless soul; he could not cope...' she seemed unsure of how to continue. '... he, well, having everything... especially after having so little as a soldier and as a prisoner in Algiers... it was too much. He also missed his daughter Isabel, with whom he had returned from Portugal; she was just a baby. Well... in the end he left... but with insight and direction. You see, he had begun to write and draw. He took back with him his first novel 'La Galatea'. I was sad to see him go.' She finished looking wistfully out onto the busy narrow street. I once again felt that inner turmoil at the knowledge of her age and the mystery of all the partners she had been with. It was unnerving. I gulped down my wine.

I wondered if she had brought me here to gently remind me. I realised she did not like to just be with people she liked to have an impact to mould them, to shape them, prepare them so that they can have an effect on their world, whether it is to stay with her or leave. I knew I could not just shut out everything and live in a bubble; that was not her way.

'I suppose you have his manuscript of that to?' I said remembering all the Ovid manuscripts. She nodded.

'Yes it is the only one although I have first editions of all his works and scripts of all his plays. They are on the shelves in our lounge.' I nodded accepting this statement. 'The manuscript I have here.' She pulled a large old leather wallet full of roughly edged papers out of her bag. I had not seen it on our whole trip so far. I leaned forward my interest getting the better of me and took it gingerly as she held it out. I remembered what had happened when I had opened Ovid's manuscript and was unsure if I wanted to go where this would send me.

'Why?' I said 'Why come here?'

'Because you mentioned him; rightly or wrongly...' she looked at me a little concerned. 'I thought I would show you the two routes that you have. You see Publius was content with me. Our path together suited him and he stayed with me until his death. It is the history that is known.' She smiled 'although the historians don't know the details as you do. Miguel, now he was different. He came to me in some confusion but stayed only a year. He had not lost his memory like you. He was restless and even when I had given him my calming draught; the pull of his new daughter was stronger. His love for her was so intense he had to return. The choice though it distressed him intensely.' She paused, sadness had entered her voice. 'His time with me though, it disappeared it is not part of the history of this world.' Suddenly she looked at me; her gaze intense. She saw deep into my soul. 'You remind me of him.'

I looked down at the manuscript on my lap.

'What's it about?' I gestured to the book.

'It will make you smile. It is a myriad of entangled relationships centred around a girl called Galatea.'

'Fits I guess.' I said, though I was not sure I wanted to smile. I was feeling a bit confused and I could not resist the manuscripts pull. This time though I was ready for what was to happen. Undoing the leather-string tie I opened up the folder in front of me, releasing hundreds of rough cut sheets of parchment. I looked down at the first one. I could make out the title underlined in faded ink 'La Galatea'. The scrawling lines beneath, I could not read. I guessed they were in Spanish. I tried to pronounce the words in my head...

Then, as before, I found myself standing in a room. Bells were ringing in the distance. A cough made me look across to a man who sat at a table by a window, writing. I could see his face, he looked weary, lines creased his forehead his hair was thin. He wore a perfectly trimmed pointed beard, so prevalent of those times. I knew it was Cervantes writing those first lines. Beyond him I could see what I guessed was the sixteenth Century town of Toledo. He turned and looked across at a dark haired woman sitting by a hearth doing needlework. She looked up and smiled at him. I was taken by surprise because the woman I saw was almost identical to the Carna I knew.

He spoke and gestured to his writing. He turned back to his table but instead of continuing he picked up a small sketch that he had propped up in front of him and stared at it. I moved closer and saw that it was a drawing of a baby's head and shoulders. I guessed it to be Isabel his daughter. He sighed and put it down again. Turning back to his writing the quill began to scratch across the page rapidly.

I looked back at the seated woman. She stood and after a quick word to Cervantes, who, head down, just nodded in reply, she beckoned me to follow. We walked out into a courtyard full of greenery. A fountain bubbled at its centre. We walked toward the entrance which was marked by two large bronze doors. She opened one of the doors. Outside I could see the bustling renaissance street, hear voices calling, shouting and animals, the clatter of hooves. Preparing myself I stepped out and found that I was back in the restaurant looking at Carna.

'It was you!' was the first thing that came to me. 'Not just you but the you that I see! You looked the same.'

'A little bit older, but yes. You see now why I said you were similar. You see me in the same way.' A thought suddenly came to me.

'The door; I didn't realise last time, you know with Ovid. I guess I was a bit too overcome by it. But anyway, I went through the other door when I left; the one that I can't open back at our house.'

'The door that leads out, to other times, to other lives.'

'I must go through that door mustn't I, if I'm going to return?' she did not answer just smiled and sipped at her wine. 'I had become content, enjoying life not thinking about it.' I mumbled.

'I know, but unfortunately you must actively choose you cannot hide from a decision. Janus will not allow it.'

'So what happens if I just ignore.'

'Continued reminders, you will not get left in peace until your decision is made. I'm sorry.' I listened to the laughter and chatter of the other people in the restaurant noting their happy contented faces. Somehow they all suddenly seemed so far away.

X

As August blended into September I found myself getting agitated. I had not been able to let go of my vision of Cervantes and Carna. It had perturbed me, whereas Ovid had not. Ovid had been content with his lot, but Cervantes, he had appeared restless, agitated, not ready to slip into a tranquil state with Carna. I found myself connecting to that. Everything was perfect but it gave me no purpose no direction. I knew I needed that. The past kept niggling at the back of my mind.

I pushed my breakfast around the plate. I could feel Carna watching me. I could sense her concern. Finally I picked up my coffee and wandered into the study and clicked on the computer. I had not looked for a long time.

My tenuous illusion of peace was finally shattered by a simple e-mail from a certain Reginald Palmer, private investigator. I sat down at the desk and clicked open. It read: 'Have found Geoff; contact me and we can arrange to meet. RIP.'

What did he mean by RIP? I was closing in on decision time. Did I want to meet this elusive Geoff who may have all the answers?

In the end the decision was easy I knew I had to meet up with Reginald and see where it led me. If I did not, not knowing the knowledge that he and Geoff had would never stop gnawing away inside me, like a parasitic worm.

I clicked on 'reply' and sent back that I would meet him the next day at the café of our previous meeting. My hand hesitated over the 'send' button just for a moment but then I pressed.

The rest of the day I spent in confusion unable to settle, going from one thing to the next, eventually collapsing exhausted into bed.

I was up early the next morning, partly through lack of sleep and waking early but I also had at the back of my mind a plan to be waiting for Reginald, to give myself a slight advantage. Carna still seemed to manage to get breakfast as usual.

Going into town I parked up and walked to the small café. It was a surprisingly cold morning. It had been a long hot summer so it was probably not as cold as it felt but I got the feeling that autumn was stirring. I pulled my jacket around me as I walked through the streets. My thoughts were interrupted by a fluttering of leaves from the roadside trees. It was as though they were disturbed by the change and chattered nervously. Hints of gold, yellow and brown would soon appear. I stopped outside the café and looked up through the canopy of the nearest tree to a thick carpet of menacing grey cloud that hung low in the sky.

With a sigh, brought on partly by my situation and partly by the changing seasons, I pushed open the café door. I was hit by a wave of humid warm air that washed over me. I found it comforting. As I stepped in I pulled my coat off noting that I was half an hour early. I scanned the room for a spare table. It was a popular café. As my eyes roamed, I noticed a hand waving. It was Reginald. He sat comfortably in a window recess. Two steaming mugs of tea were on the table a plate of biscuits between them. I walked over surprised and slightly deflated that he had beaten me.

'Morning Francis. Good to see you. Was beginning to wonder when I'd hear from you. Thought you might have given up on the hunt, so to speak,' He chuckled.

Biscuit crumbs fell from his moustache onto his blazer. He brushed them away, 'sorry can't have a cup of tea without a biscuit.'

'You're early.' I blurted out without thinking. He smiled.

'So are you.' Realising how I must have sounded I mumbled an apology.

'Sit down. Here I have got you a tea.' I sat, feeling a little bemused. It must have shown on my face. 'Saw you coming.' He pointed through the window.

'Why so early though?' I had not quite moved on.

'Oh I like to stay one step ahead...' he laughed, 'Biscuit?' he said, picking up the plate and holding it in front of me.

'Err, no thank you.' He just nodded and took one for himself. I realised I had underestimated this man when I had first met him. I sipped the tea; it was good, strong; the way I liked it, although this early I would have preferred a coffee as I felt a need for caffeine.

'You've found him then...' Reginald nodded, picking up another biscuit, dunking it in his tea and noisily munching. More crumbs powdered his moustache which he again brushed with his fingers. He finished the biscuit before replying.

'Yes reasonably straight forward actually.' He rummaged in a small old leather briefcase by the side of his chair. 'Here.' He passed across a plastic file. I flicked it open. There was a photo on the first page. 'Is that him?' I studied the photo of a man just stepping down the front steps of a town house. He was smartly dressed and carried a brief case in one hand. I had no memory of Geoff so did not quite know how to respond. So I just grunted and leaned forward studying the photo in more detail. 'Here.'

Reginald dug into his blazer pocket and pulled out a magnifying glass.

'Quite the Sherlock Holmes, I see,' I said and, 'thanks,' as I took the magnifier. Looking through it I studied the man. His hair was cut very short to compensate for it being very thin on top. He looked in his thirties. He was tanned and looked fit and healthy, carrying no extra weight. His features looked rather sharp. His chin pointed, nose thin. He looked like a man who was confident and content with his situation. I studied the rest of the picture, to see if I could recognise where it was. I guessed that the house in the background belonged to the man as he was exiting with an air of propriety. It was a tall Georgian style house in a long terrace. The area looked affluent. The house looked as though it had just been painted. There were no signs of wear and tear to be seen in the picture.

My gaze was drawn to the entrance; A large front door which was just behind the man. It somehow looked familiar. I moved the magnifying glass up and down to improve the definition and leant right down over the picture. It was a large door coated in green oxidised copper. I gasped as I recognised the patterns upon it.

'You ok?' came a muffled voice. I looked up at Reginald who was busy finishing off the biscuits. 'You look a bit pale.'

'No I'm ok.' I said trying to give him a smile which I guessed was more of a grimace. I quickly looked back down at the picture; seeing again the large bronze door knocker with the two faces of Janus. It was identical to the doors at Carna's house. Except there was only one!

'It's him. It has to be!' I blurted out.

'Well that's good then.' Reginald replied. 'Read the rest of the report, it won't take you long and I'm not in any hurry.' He said, his eyes twinkling as he reached for another biscuit and dunked it in his tea.

Putting down the magnifying glass I turned the page. My tea still untouched, I began to read. 'Geoffrey Price aged 38 lives at 81 Kings Way, London with his wife Patricia and child Emily aged 8. He has lived at this address since January last year. He works for Hamlet Consultancies, where he is a senior executive. He has no financial issues. He has two cars both new. Patricia does not work.' I absentmindedly picked up my semi-cold tea and sipped it as I mulled over the information.

'Did you happen to discover anything about his past?' I queried.

'I didn't really look too hard at that. After all you just asked me to find him.' He smiled, 'But his birth certificate, of which you have a copy... next page.' I turned over and studied it. '...shows that he came from Sheffield. Marriage certificate... next...' He gestured, I turned again, '...shows he married here nine years ago.' I was suitably impressed.

'That's excellent, thank you, you have done very well.'

'Why thank you, always good to receive a compliment.' He hesitated for a moment and then reached over and turned to the next page, 'My bill.' He pointed. I choked a little at the sum, until I remembered that my funds seemed at present to appear limitless, my bank account always seemed to have the same amount in it no matter how much we spent.

'Cheque do?' He nodded and I proceeded to fill it in.

'Thank you.' Taking the cheque, Reg tucked it into his blazer and rose from his seat. 'You know where I am if you need any further use of my services.' I nodded, standing too. He shook my hand, 'it's been a pleasure.' I held on to his hand.

'Before you go... RIP, what did you mean?' After a moment's confusion Reginald broke out into a huge guffaw.

'Oh...' He spluttered struggling to speak, 'You mean on the e-mail.' I nodded. 'Yes that well don't worry it's not Rest In Peace, just Reginald Ignatius Palmer. RIP you see my initials!' He guffawed again. 'Well goodbye old chap and good luck with...' he pointed at the file and then turning headed for the door.

I watched him go and then sat down, picking up the file once again. This time I read through some of the detail that I had skipped earlier. I noticed a set of phone numbers, a land line and a mobile. My heart began to beat faster as I mulled over the possibility of giving them a try.

I pulled out my mobile and put it in front of me on the table. I knew that by ringing I could potentially change everything. Flashes of first Carna then Ovid and Cervantes dashed through my thoughts. Finally, with shaking hand I picked up the phone and began to dial. The land line rang out with no answer. I guessed at this time of day mid-week they were all out. I dialled the mobile number.

'Hello Geoffrey Price speaking.' I did not recognise the voice but did not expect to. I now had confirmation that the man on the step was the man I was looking for. I felt my heart pounding but did not know what to say. 'Hello...'

'Err... Hello Geoffrey, my name is Francis, Francis Smith...' I heard a sharp intake of breath. He did not reply. For a moment there was silence so I carried on. 'I was wondering...' the phone line had been cut. I sat back with a sigh, feeling my tense muscles slowly relax. I did not know what to make of it, or what I should do. It was obvious that he did not want contact; that hearing me had spooked him. I opened up the file again and studied his picture, memorising the face.

I was finally disturbed from my reverie by the polite cough of the waitress who presented me with the bill for the tea and biscuits. I looked at my semi full mug of now cold tea and the empty plate of biscuits next to Reginald's drained mug.

'The old fox!' I muttered

'Pardon me sir?' the waitress took a step back and watched me nervously.

'Oh nothing, sorry …here…' I reached into my pocket and pulled out a ten pound note. Of late I had noticed that there always seemed to be one there. 'Keep the change.' This brought a smile back to her face.

I gathered up the file and headed out of the stuffy café into the autumn air.

For the next few days his face never left my thoughts. I could not settle. I swam and walked until I was exhausted. I fished, cycled, even visited the Coach and Horses but made a quick exit out of the back entrance after one drink when I noticed the neighbours Peter and Valerie coming in and did not want to get into any conversation with them.

Returning to the house that evening I was soon pacing up and down the living room, an empty glass in my hand, unable to sit, relax and let go.

Carna sat curled up like a cat. Her bright blue eyes glistening in the light of the log fire, following me until I could ignore them no more. I stopped and looked across at her, as always slightly in awe of the immense beauty and the power that seemed to exude from her. She drew my eyes to hers, the corners of her mouth rose slightly in a half smile and I felt my agitation slip away slightly.

'Go see him,' she purred, 'you know that you want to.' She saw my hesitation, uncertainty. I felt as though she had sneaked into my soul. I felt a shiver run through me. I had not mentioned my visit to Reginald or the fact that I had discovered Geoff. 'Just speak to him. You don't have to make any decisions.' I looked at her, my surprise evident. Walking over to the decanter I filled my glass. It gave me time to think.

'Why?' I turned to face her. 'Why are you telling me this?' I did not question how she knew. I just accepted that she knew everything.

'You will not be content until you have seen him.' I knew she was right. 'Besides, you need to see him to decide. And you must decide.' The last comment she said more forcefully and I could feel the echo of Janus in her voice. For an instant it chilled me, even though I stood next to the roaring fire. I nodded. It seemed the only thing to do.

'Good, tomorrow then?'

'Ok.'

'That's settled now perhaps you can sit down.' She smiled and I found myself melting before her, sitting without even realising.

Carna woke me early the next morning and after a quick croissant and coffee drove me to the local train station. I waved as she drove off, feeling a bit bemused. Wandering into the station I purchased a first class ticket to Euston. It was no surprise to see the high speed train waiting in the station. Carna had wanted me to go so my journey would be a smooth one. I boarded the train and sat down in the first class compartment, glad that I had paid the extra as the train was heaving with commuters. Not that I had any concern for the cost of things at this time.

Arriving at Euston station I walked up the ramps and into the foyer. It was a place of frenzy. Suited commuters, case carrying travellers of all nations milled and moved with purpose, intent on their personal private and important journeys. I stood and allowed the movement to flow around me, getting my bearings and deciding on my next move.

Strangely I could remember the station; A memory that must have emerged from my past. I wondered at its selectivity. Was I or Janus for that matter blocking certain things? I knew where to go to catch the tube so once again joined the throng, like a mass of wood ants milling about their nest. I walked across the large open space my eyes constantly focused on the movement all around so that I did not hit anyone and could find the easiest route across to the escalator that lead down into the underbelly of London; a strange detached world of continuous movement. I had planned my tube journey on the train earlier, so headed through the turnstiles and followed the signs for the Northern Line running south to the Embankment. From there I headed west on the District Line towards Wimbledon. The train's occupants slowly thinned as it left the centre of town and I found myself a seat. At Twickenham I disembarked and was glad to breathe fresh air outside the station.

I walked slowly along the traffic laden roads towards my destination becoming more hesitant and reluctant as I went. Finally I turned off the busy highway and left behind the noise and busyness as I walked into a suburban tree lined street. I counted off the house numbers as I walked down eventually stopping outside number 81. I had recognised it even from a distance. The large distinctive green door stood out and as I got closer the two headed door knocker became more defined.

I looked up and down the street. It was quiet, apart from a cat that sat on the pavement watching me. There was no distraction to delay me so I pushed open the gate, the steady rhythm of my heart increasing with every step. I reached out and grabbed the circular ring of the door handle. It suddenly occurred to me that there may be nobody in; it was after all the middle of the day. It was a possibility that I had not thought of.

The cat meowed and I turned to look at it as it sat at the gate. Its strange blue eyes stared at me. A flash vision of Carna standing before me made me focus and with a deep breath I turned and banged down the knocker. I heard movement inside as I knew I would. Carna would not have allowed me to come if there was no one in; the thought made me smile.

The door was opened by a middle aged blonde haired woman. She was well made up, slightly tanned and elegantly dressed.

'Hello can I help you?'

'Err Hello; Yes I would like to speak with Geoff please?' She smiled

'You know Geoff. Who shall I say is calling?'

'Francis'

'Ok, hang on a moment.' She wandered back into the house leaving the door open. I looked in to a modern carpeted hallway. I could hear her talking deeper in the house. She reappeared looking concerned and confused. Her face flushed through her tan as she said,

'Err... he seems to have gone out, can I take a message?' It was my moment to be confused.

'I have come a long way. Are you sure…?'

'He's not in.' She was becoming agitated.

'I thought I heard his voice.' I said looking past her. She stepped across my field of view.

'No;' she looked sternly at me, 'Any message?'

'Well… tell him Francis Smith called. I would like to meet up with him again.'

'Ok Good-bye.' She went to close the door. I felt my emotions rise, I was becoming desperate. I could not face the thought of leaving without seeing him; surely Carna would not allow that. The cat meowed behind me. Without thinking I pushed my hand into the closing door and then let out a roar of pain as it crushed my fingers. She pulled it open and looked at me her face pale and shocked. Blood dripped from my fingers.

'Gosh, sorry I didn't mean to…' I shook my head feeling the sharpness of the pain slowly fade to be replaced by a dull numbness in my fingers and a throbbing ache in my hand. I pulled out my handkerchief and tried to wrap it around my hand.

'No, my fault,' I stuttered. 'It's just…' I looked up into her concerned eyes. Her previous anger had momentarily abated. 'I need to see him Patricia. I cannot bear to leave without seeing him. Please talk to him again.' She looked at me slightly surprised; I guessed because I had used her name. She took a moment to compose herself.

'He was insistent; he did not want to see you.' I caught a glimpse of movement behind her down the hall and guessed whoever was there was listening.

'Look,' I pleaded, cradling my bleeding hand. 'Tell him I forgive him, I just need him to answer some questions to help me move on.'

'Forgive him, move on! What do you mean forgive him? For what?'

'Could you just ask him how he would feel if our situations were reversed?'

'You are talking in riddles. Look I am sorry about your hand but I need to close the door. Please move back.' She began to once again shut the door. I backed down the steps slowly feeling lost.

'Patricia!' I stopped in the mid-step, holding my breath. The door had not quite closed. 'Open it;' this was said more quietly, calmly and with determination. I recognised Geoff's voice.

'But Geoffrey, you said...' I could hear her moving from the door. She had not closed it but not opened it any further either. 'You said... well you know what you said. What is going on? Who is he?'

'I'll try to explain later, but I will have to see him. He won't give up. He will just keep trying until he does see me so I might as well see him now.' I heard her give a dissatisfied grunt and move off down the corridor. Then the door slowly swung open.

'Hello Francis.' I looked at the man before me, Taking in his features more clearly now than I had been able to in the small photograph. Thin sharp face, ferret like, balding hair brushed back to hide the loss. He was slim and healthy, well dressed in designer slacks and v necked sweater. 'So you found me. I thought you would eventually but it hasn't taken you as long as I expected.' He stood watching me and I him; both of us unsure of the next move. I could feel my heart racing and wondered if he was feeling the same; I was full of nervous apprehension now that I was finally face to face with him.

'Well I guess you had better come in.' He stepped aside and I entered the house, the Janus door closing behind me. 'This way;' He had opened a door into the front room. I heard a noise and saw Patricia watching us from the end of the corridor. Her arms crossed and brow furrowed in agitation.

'Patricia dear, could you make some tea, please.' She nodded and reluctantly disappeared. I walked into a comfortable front living room, white walls, fire place, wooden floor, and sat in a rather uncomfortable modern chair. Geoff sat opposite me and once again we fell into an uncomfortable silence. Eventually, after a furtive look at the door Geoff said, 'how is she?' I stared at him confused.

'Who?'

'Carna of course.'

'Oh, Carna, yes I see. Much the same I guess for a demi-goddess nymph who is thousands of years old.'

'I guess so, although from what I remember of that last night, my Carna wasn't your Carna.' I looked at him once again confused. He tried to explain, 'my Carna didn't look like the one you saw. Mine was blonde yours brunette I believe.'

'Ah, yes she is different to each beholder. I have seen that but I don't remember that night.' It was his turn to look bemused. Before he could question me the door swung open and Patricia entered with a tray. She held it out and I took a mug of tea. I mumbled a 'thanks'. Geoff took a mug and then Patricia, after a look at her husband left again.

'You don't remember?'

'No, I do not even remember you. At some point after that night I fell…, lost my memory. I don't think that was part of the plan. Carna also gave me a brew, or some sort of concoction as well that seemed to subdue me, I think.'

'Carna's medication; Yes I remember that.' Geoff sighed. 'I remember how it lifts you out of all your troubles, makes everything right, makes you feel on top of the world.' He smiled. 'The troubles of the world are easy to forget when you are with a goddess. Don't get me wrong I am glad I have returned so to speak but there is much that I remember… It's strange to have everything but somehow… well the memories of my past, I could not let them go. They tormented me, but you… you say you lost your memory. How come you have found me? How come you are searching? Surely you would have just sort of settled into a … well …perfect existence.'

'That's the thing; it's not perfect is it? There is something unreal about it. I found myself yearning for my memories. The past I did not have. The more I have learned the more my emotions have been in turmoil.' I looked out of the window as two teenagers walked past talking loudly. 'Sometimes I would hide from it but always it would creep in. It has been nine months now.' Geoff nodded at me, his head continued to bob as he absorbed what I said and thought. I could see he was half listening to me half reflecting on his own experiences. Finally he replied.

'It took me three years before I finally left.' I held my breath not wanting to disturb his thoughts. 'At first all was fuzzy; Carna and her potions. Then I went through a turmoil of memory, I followed that with acceptance and… yes … enjoyment. But they came back, those memories.'

'Janus.'

'Yes, you cannot just accept; you must face it and make a decision and until you do…' he looked at me; his eyes seeing into me. 'Well I think you understand.' I nodded.

'Part of me would love to just accept, but...I keep getting flashbacks of my family.'

'So you remember some things? You remembered me?'

'Not exactly; I wrote some notes in a book before I collapsed. You were in there with a description of what had happened that night. You know, me coming with you to your house...' I gave him a hard stare at that. His face reddened. I pulled out my small notebook. It was quite full now from my constant jottings, but the first page was the most thumbed and tired looking, as over the last nine months I had constantly read through those first nine questions that I had written before I had lost my memory. Turning to the first page I read: *'Everything had changed when I arrived with Geoff at his house. Note-need to find Geoff.'*

'Is that it?' I held out the book for him, taking it I watched his eyes move slowly down the page.

'That's it nine thoughts that I wrote before I lost my memory; plus the information about coming to the house, research on Ovid and Janus...' He flicked through the small rather tattered book.

'Rosie, Theresa and Michael, I knew you had a family; I did not want to think about them. I never knew their names. It was hard enough doing what I had to do.' He looked away not wanting to hold my gaze. I did not answer him, even though I wanted to shout angrily into his face. I knew he had more to say and I needed to hear. 'You had to have a family you see, some sort of tie... otherwise it would not have worked.' Before I could ask him what he

171

meant he said. 'How did you find me though, just from this?' He flicked through the pages in the note book.

'It gave me your first name,' I explained. 'I found your full name from colleagues at work. Then I hired a Private Investigator.' His head bobbed, 'and well here I am.'

'So what now?' I thought for a moment.

'The notebook, it talks about my coming to the house with you but it is a bit confusing.' I took it from him and turned to the relevant description and read it out. 'Entered the house with Geoff, through left hand door, it was dark, he introduced me to his wife then left by the right hand door. It was light outside that door! He said on leaving - *Sorry Francis. You are a good man. It has to be this way. In time you will understand.* I have tried to open that right hand door it will not budge. What actually happened?' He leaned forward in his chair and looked at the floor; his hands clasped together, thumbs rotating nervously around each other.

'Yes New Year's Eve...' he looked up at me, emotion in his moist eyes; 'and I truly am sorry but I had to find someone you understand. This curse it moves from one to the next. If you want to get out you must find a replacement.'

'Replacement!' I almost shouted, he nodded. There was movement at the door and we turned as it opened. Patricia looked in concern on her face.

'I heard...' she looked about suspiciously, 'raised voices.'

'It's ok love.'

'Are you ok Geoffrey? You look as...' He stopped her by raising his hand.

'Yes, I'm fine.' She made a move to come in. He stood up to intercept her and took her hands in his 'Patricia, my dear, I am ok really but I need to…' He was unsure how to phrase his need for her to leave without upsetting her. 'We need to,' he gestured towards me; 'we need to finish our conversation. Just the two of us…' I could see the hurt in her eyes. She stared from her husband to me, then back to him. 'Please…' he pleaded. She nodded and then with a final glance at me, left. He sat back down. My thoughts turned back to our conversation and what he had told me.

'She told me there had been many but I thought we had been picked by her or by Janus. I did not think.' I shook my head not wanting to accept the full implication of Geoff's statement.

'Yes it is for each to pick his successor. Janus of course has the final say, so if you get it wrong the door will not open.' We were silent for a moment. Then Geoff mumbled 'It is his last cruel twist, Janus's that is; you escape but as a betrayer to a friend. I have suffered so much guilt this last nine months. I refused to do it initially, when I had worked out what had to be done that is. For over a year I fought with my conscience. Janus plays with you though. The more I fought it, the more it hurt me, the more candidates would appear. I did not ask for you to talk to me. I even tried to warn you off but you were persistent. In the end… well I could resist no longer.' I picked up on one part of what he had said.

'You said you had worked out what had to be done.' He nodded.

'Yes, take the person you wish to swap with in the left hand door and exit through the right hand door. It will open for you if the person you bring is accepted. The right hand door returns you to your previous existence. You have to do this on the last day of the year.' My mind was swamped by what I had learned.

'To escape I must find someone to take my place.' I mumbled out loud. I watched as he nodded, stood and headed across to a drinks cabinet.

'Do you like whisky?' It was my turn to nod absently at him. 'Funny thing is I never used to like the stuff and well since then; now I do. Aqua Vitae!' He chuckled and poured out two tumblers full and handed me one. My mind was still mulling over what I would need to do.

'Or I could stay.'

'That is the other choice you have. Although even that is time limited.'

'Yes, she told me, nineteen years. I feel like a piece on a gaming board.' I said gulping the smooth single malt.

'I think that is how it is. Janus sitting up with the other gods laughing and drinking as they play.'

'She says he is weak; now not able to leave the ruined temples and statues that are left.' He looked at me surprised.

'Is that so; yet the game goes on.'

'He may not leave his ruined temples but he is still able to reach out and play the game. I think it is his life line now. He will not let it stop. Indeed Carna herself does not want it to end. It keeps her immortal. She would die if it ended.'

'You have learned quite a lot from her.' Geoff mumbled. He had not sat down but stood swirling the amber liquid in his glass as he gazed absently through the windows. 'The game, it plays on our human weakness. I think it is in man's destiny never to be content. To have

174

everything but want something else, to feel that there is something we haven't achieved or should be striving for. To want what we haven't got then when we get it to miss what we have given up; to endlessly search.' He gave a cynical chuckle and gulped down his whisky. 'I have come to wonder if that perhaps we do not really need or want any of it, for all it is, is a distraction.'

'Perhaps we need that distraction So that we don't have to face the enormity of not knowing what life is all about.'

'It has made us into philosophers!' he turned and faced me, alert to my expression. 'Can you forgive me?'

'What, for sending me there.' I gave a half-hearted laugh. 'I should not.' I sipped my whisky watching him. His face fell. 'But I have to don't I.' He looked at me sharply, his brow knitted together in concern.

'How so?'

'Well if I don't forgive you how can I go and do the same if that is to be the choice I decide to make.'

'Is it?' I could see he was holding his breath desperate for release from the suffering his guilt had given him; the legacy of being a pawn in the game.

'I don't know. Sometimes I have a great yearning to see it, that past, but at others... well I think I was driven with a greater urgency because I had no memory but it also means I have nothing concrete to base my decisions on. It seems I have come to understand it all quicker than most but now I don't know what to do.' I swigged down the last of my whisky. 'What I do know is I seem to drink a heck of a lot of this stuff.' Geoff smiled.

'Me too.' He got the bottle and filled our glasses.

'So you can forgive me? It's just that well I returned but what I did has haunted me since then…' He would have carried on but I raised my hand to stop him.

'As I said Geoff, I have to forgive you and I do.' He collapsed into a chair.

'You are releasing me from his hold. Even when I left…' he gestured around the room. 'Things, material things, work all went well, I seemed to get everything I wanted but I could not get the release from my conscience. Thank you, a great weight has been lifted.' I nodded thoughtfully and watched him get up and pace the room, wanting to be free myself and yet not understanding where that freedom actually was. What I knew though was that holding a grudge against this man before me was not going to change anything. I could not feel anger towards him because I could not remember!

He stopped his pacing and looked at me.

'Now all I'm left with is my infidelity.' He gave a wry smile. 'How do I tell my wife I spent three years living with a goddess when to her, I never left home?' He took a large gulp from his glass. I shrugged; I could see no answer to this and as I sipped at my own drink I pondered that if I returned, I too would have this dilemma.

'So what are you going to do now?'

'I don't know,' I replied after a moment's hesitation. 'Go back; think on what we have said.' I held up my hands and shrugged.

'You will have to decide, to stay or go, you cannot just sit on the fence. Janus won't allow it.'

'I know, it's not part of the rules! I cannot decide not just yet. I have to get my head round all this. Then, well then we'll see.' I stood up and finished the last of my second whisky. I felt a little bit fuzzy. 'I best go; I think I had better get some fresh air to walk off those drinks, clear my head and do some thinking. Geoff nodded sagely towards me. He was now relaxed and somehow changed; the lines on his forehead had gone as had the early nervous agitated movements. He was free I reminded myself. Free from the game.

I left with a promise to come back and see him when I had either managed to return or if I decided to stay and soon found myself wandering the streets of London rather aimlessly.

My meanderings took me down to the banks of the Thames, where I soon wandered into a park, formal gardens laid with colourful flower beds, the hum of insects dashing eagerly between the late blooms mingled with the constant hum of traffic. I came upon a small circular pond, orange and white fish came lazily to the surface as I stared down at my green tinged reflection. Noticing a small foot bridge to my right I wandered up onto it to be greeted by the view of a magnificent Georgian brick mansion.

I was tempted to wander across to it and explore but the sound of running water drew me back down to the circular pond. I looked in the direction of the sound through the manicured lawns and squared off yew hedges. At the end of the lawn I was surprised to see what appeared to be a marble statue atop some rocks with water falling over them.

As I approached the rocks, waterfall and pool beneath became an idyllic magical grotto populated with 7 naked marble female figures. On top of the rockery a further naked female stood astride two winged horses, water cascaded down into a dark pool at the base full of lush green aquatic plants and Lily flowers. I walked over to the plaque and read:

'You are in the riverside part of York House Gardens looking at the sculptures carved in the renowned Italian white marble of Carrara. They represent the Oceanides, or sea nymphs of Greek mythology and although we cannot be sure of the name of the sculptor it seems that they came from the Roman Studio of Orazio Andreoni at the turn of the nineteenth century.'

I suddenly had a suspicion that I had been led here. I felt Carna's hand in this. These powerful and captivating marble figures gleaming white in the afternoon sun were I felt sure not Greek nymphs but Roman and portrayed one in particular. Even the fact that their origin was in doubt made me certain that here was another representation of Carna. Taking out my notebook I wrote down the name of the possible sculptor and was determined to do a bit more digging. Looking again at the figures I marvelled at the human contortions that they held and yet the somehow divine look that they expressed; the human goddess, yes that was Carna all over.

I sat down on a bench in front of them and soaked up the atmosphere that they evoked. The sound of the waterfall slowly eroded my stress. I began to relax and the tension of the last few hours evaporated, allowing me to order my thoughts. I smiled to myself; I was sure the statues were watching me. Taking out my notebook I wrote down everything that had happened to me that day.

XI

On my return I found Carna waiting, a meal on the table, wine in the glasses. I raised my glass, tasting the light Italian fruitiness of the Red and looked into her deep blue eyes. She asked how my day had gone and yet I knew she already knew.

'Yes I found him and I learned what I needed to know although I discovered nothing that made me leap for joy. Although I'm sure you know what I discovered.' She smiled and reached over taking my hand. I felt the anger that had been growing inside me evaporate. We ate in silence. I did not see the need to fill her in on the day as she knew and would add nothing more to what I had found out. A vision of the statues, finally made me speak.

'Who was Orazio Andreoni then?' A knowing smile lifted the corners of her perfect mouth.

'Orazio, he was a sculptor; had a studio in Italy. Did very well a hundred years ago selling sculptures to the Anglo-American market.'

'You sound like an encyclopaedia or a saleswoman. Was he one of your men?' I said roughly. She looked down at her half-finished meal and shook her head. Her dark long lustrous Mediterranean hair glistened in the light of the candles that she had lit in the dining room. Women went to great lengths to create the look and poise that she had naturally I mused. Even when I was agitated I could not take my eyes off her. Each move she made seemed to caress my soul.

'No he was not one of my men as you put it.'

'You knew him though?' she nodded watching me intently; letting me find my way. 'Those sculptures at York House in London?'

'Did you like them?'

'Yes, you know I did.' With a sudden flash of inspiration I almost shouted out, 'They are you!'

'Yes they are.' This time I did not say anything and waited for her to explain. It took some moments but finally she consented.

'I was with a sculptor called Oscar Spalmach at the time. He worked at Andreoni's studio.' She paused to take a breath. 'It is strange; Oscar never saw me as just one person as you do and all the others. I guess it was the artist in him; there was not just one perfection, for him perfection was constantly evolving; it was ever changing and therefore so was I. With each new face he carved another statue. Their positioning at York House is not how he envisaged them ending up but it is evocative all the same.'

'So they are not portraying Oceanides.'

'No although it is a good enough interpretation and there have been a few. Venus stands above on the pair of Hippocampi….'

'Sorry, What?'

'Hippocampi, they are sort of water horses. Though, even she is me.'

'Who, Venus?'

'Yes, Oscar wanted to portray his fight, the battle in every man's soul perhaps, that between lust and love, the nymphs versus Venus.'

'Ah I see now, very poignant; His fight between the temptations of Carna, the seven temptations in the case of this statue and of his love of whoever his Venus was in his parallel world. I suppose even the number seven has meaning!'

'Actually yes; He was a catholic. To him the number seven did have significance and one fitting to the meaning he was trying to achieve.' She stopped and took a mouthful of lasagne.

'Go on.' I muttered prompting her to continue.

'Well there are the seven deadly sins as laid down by Pope Gregory in the sixth century – lust of course, pride, envy, sloth, wrath and gluttony. These are balanced by the seven Holy virtues of chastity, temperance, charity, diligence, patience, kindness and humility.'

'Well here's to Oscar!' I raised my glass cynically and drank. 'Another poor victim; though I have to admit he has created a classic there; Once seen not forgotten.' I became morose and quiet after that. I was tired of hearing her talk of other men that she had known and yet I could see exactly what Oscar was portraying; I could feel it in my soul. As soon as I could I headed to the study and read through my notes.

It was late when I finally succumbed to the exhaustion of a long day. I had sat in the office trying to see a way forward; trying to understand the feelings that I seemed to be constantly driving me onward.

Geoff's words kept going round in my head so much so that I found myself writing them over and over in the little book. I read them over one last time'... *I think it is in man's destiny never to be content. To have everything but want something else, to feel that there is something we haven't achieved or should be striving for. To want what we haven't got then when we get it to miss what we have given up; to endlessly search...*' I felt incomplete. That I decided was my reason but I still did not know how to proceed. I felt I could not knowingly take someone else out of their contented life and use them as a pawn for my escape. I saw the haunted look in Geoff's eyes when he first saw me and the relief when I had forgiven him. I knew I would feel the same. Putting the book into the drawer, I shuffled exhausted to the bedroom and to the sleeping outline of Carna.

I found my sleep broken by a trail of men stepping out of a white mist; led first by men in Roman dress, togas and military uniforms; amongst these I recognised Ovid who paused and looked deeply into my eyes; then onwards into varied European costumes of the dark ages, one after another they stepped past me, traders, warriors, clergy. Then on into the Middle Ages, this time I recognised Cervantes who stopped and gave me a nod and wry smile. As the night wore on the line of men continued one after another to step out of the mist and walk off into the distance. I saw a Pope and at least one King, beggars too dressed in rags, there seemed no definition of rank or wealth. After some time a dusty man in overalls stopped, I could see his dress beneath was distinctly nineteenth century. I heard myself say 'Oscar Spalmach?' he smiled sadly and nodded before continuing. The last to step out of the mist was Geoff. He raised his hand and bobbed his head encouragingly, then trudged on behind the others. The line stretched on into the distance but as they walked Geoff did not seem to get any further away.

Next morning as I tried to wash away the city's stickiness and the restless night with a swim in the pool Carna entered; pulling off her nightdress she stood for a moment allowing my eyes to devour her then with a grin dived perfectly into the cool waters, leaving hardly a ripple. She came up next to me and put her arms around me.

'Good morning Francis.' I could feel the pressure of her body against mine. 'So you have contemplated and thought much about what you have found out. What is it to be?' She purred. I found it difficult to think, to focus on the question she had asked. It irked me to have to think and not enjoy the scent and closeness of her flesh. But she would not let it go and when I had not replied she continued, 'well?'

Irritably I found myself pushing her away and swimming to the other side of the pool. Grabbing the side, I turned and looked across at her, a picture of perfection. Her body was that of a goddess physically perfect in every way and yet her mind, I knew was frozen and hardened by time.

'You are perfect, everything a man could want and yet I cannot stop myself wondering; I cannot stop myself wanting to search out the past. I don't think I can be content here, not forever, not even for nineteen years, and yet at the same time I cannot put someone through the turmoil of ...' I was momentarily lost for words, '...of the game.'

'You will have to decide eventually; you know that.' I nodded sadly, but I am not ready yet.' I could see she understood.

'Okay but you understand he will keep testing you.' I nodded. The next moment she disappeared under the water and came up next to me once again her arms wrapped tightly around me her lips to my ear as she whispered seductively. 'I shall say no more for now then,' she finished. Unable to resist the powers of lust, I pulled her to me.

Next morning Carna gave a large yawn and sipped at her coffee across the breakfast table.

'I have not had enough sleep.' She smiled.

'That was your fault.' I said crunching on my toast.

'It takes two.' I could not argue with that. She took another sip of her coffee. 'Guess what is special about Saturday;' she continued. I looked up caught off guard slightly, wondering what new twist was now coming. My feeling of contentment slipped away to be replaced by nervousness.

'Well today is the 29th , Michaelmas, so if I remember right, which isn't one of my strong points by the way, there are thirty days in September so that will make it the 2nd October.' She sipped at her coffee; her eyes teased me. She was in no hurry to let me in on this new adventure. 'I'm afraid that's all I can tell you about Saturday. You'll have to enlighten me.'

'You don't want to try and guess?' she pouted at me across the table.

'Sorry am I ruining your game. Now let me see; you've had your festival. Janus perhaps...?' I said facetiously; she shook her head, her smile fading. 'No, silly me January is named after him so his special days must be around there. Something to do with your god parents; now what were they called? Cybele and Alernus, that was it. I guess they are my in-laws.' I croaked out a cynical laugh.

'No, it is not my parents.' Her forehead had creased in annoyance. She stood up and started to tidy away some of the breakfast things. 'It's your birthday!' I was about to sip my coffee; my hand began to shake, so I quickly put the cup down without taking a sip. I was caught out, surprised. It had not crossed my mind in the last ten months. I realised I did not actually know how old I was.

'My birthday,' I stuttered back in reply. She nodded watching me 'I had not thought about...' Seeing my distress she came over to me and put her arm across my shoulder. I looked up at her, my recent attempts to goad her forgotten. 'How old...?' I mumbled.

'Thirty-four,' I just nodded unable now to reply, my mind working hard to digest this news. I had thirty-four years of past that I could not remember. I looked at my hand resting on the table; it was still shaking. Carna moved behind me her hands resting gently on my shoulders. 'Your parents are coming, and your brother and his family.' It took a moment for this to sink in.

'Parents! You said I was an orphan! You told me I was fostered...' I had jumped up and turned to face her, my brow furrowed with anger. 'Why?' Her shoulders had sagged; she shrugged.

'You didn't need them then.'

'And I do now?' She nodded.

'The game changes.' I said collapsing back into the chair. They were not needed then but now they are. I remembered Geoff saying that the candidates kept coming. Was that what was about to happen. I found myself leaning heavily on the table.

'My brother has a family?' I had not remembered my parents saying anything when I had visited.

'Yes, he has a wife and two children.' I was afraid to ask my next question but knew I must continue. I pulled Carna round so that I could look at her.

'And what are their names?' As I looked into her eyes, I realised I already knew the answers. I felt faint and shook my head, my grip on Carna's arms tightening. I saw her wince but could not stop myself. 'Tell me!'

'You know.' She mumbled.

185

'I want you to tell me!' my voice raised and shouting. She turned her head and looked out of the window. In a barely audible whisper she replied.

'Michael and Theresa, His children are Michael and Theresa.'

'And his wife?'

'Rosanna.'

Of course Rosanna,' I repeated, my voice full of sarcasm and released her arms. She rubbed them. They had reddened from my pressure. I felt the guilt at my actions pushing against my anger. 'Sorry.' She sat down opposite me and picked up her coffee. The red wheals from my fingers had totally disappeared. 'They're gone; did you actually feel anything.' She nodded her head. I could see her eyes were glistening with emotion. 'Sorry.' I said again and looked down at my breakfast plate. 'Are they going to stay?' I forced myself to look up into those absorbing eyes.

'No, they are just coming for lunch.'

Saturday soon arrived and Carna produced a small perfectly wrapped box at breakfast.

'Your present, Happy Birthday.' I could not help but feel pleased that she had got me something and was intrigued as to what she would give me.

I carefully removed the wrapping and opened the box to reveal a small silver medallion attached to a leather thong. It looked like an old coin. Looking closely I made out the head of a woman in profile, her long hair flowing down her neck. She was wearing a crown of sorts. I turned it over; there appeared on this alternate side a casket which appeared transparent, inside of which an oval shape was discernible. I turned back to the face and studied the words around the edge. It was not easy to read but I was sure I could make out *Magna Mater*.

'Thank you; it is your mother?'

'Yes, a coin made to commemorate her arrival in Rome.' She reached over and turned the coin over. 'That is the casket in which they brought the Black Stone from Pessino in Greece.' I nodded remembering her explanation, back in June, of the Stone that now sat in the lounge on the book case. Strangely, considering the feeling it gave upon touching it, I had not thought about it at all, it was just there… part of the house. I felt an urge to go and touch it once again. I was about to rise but Carna diverted me by placing her hands upon my shoulders. She then took the medallion from me and put it around my neck. 'There,' she said; 'she is the earth mother. Her spirit pervades all life, so perhaps this will help you to feel that spirit and gain from that strength when you need it.' She leaned round and kissed me.

I felt awkward as I opened the door to my parents later on that day. I had realised, in the intervening days since Carna had mentioned they were coming, that there had been no visitors to the house since I had lost my memory, not even my family.

My father led the way in and shook my hand. He was a tall slim bearded man, standoffish in his approach. He walked on past me, pecking Carna on the check. My mother by contrast was shorter than me, roundish and always smiling. She hugged me close.

'It seems so long since we have seen you my darling.' She muttered into my ear. 'You're looking a bit pale and thin.'

My brother came next, about my height; he appeared, solemn and serious. I guessed his edginess was due to my memory loss and the fact that we had not seen each other for some time. I took his hand and patted him on the arm. My focus already moving towards his wife, Rosanna and the two children; I had nervously awaited their arrival in fear that they would be the family that I had seen in my dreams. To my surprise Rosanna was a flaming redhead, her long hair reaching down her back, her face was freckled; her pale green eyes sparkled. She grabbed me with enthusiasm and pulled me towards her. Over her shoulder I observed the two shy children, who stood staring at the large doors.

'Strange aren't they.' I said over Rosanna's shoulder.

'He's scary,' piped the girl pointing at the large door knocker.

'Yes,' I replied as Rosanna let me go. 'He scares me too.'

'Why don't you take it off then?' queried the boy giving me a direct look.

'If I take that off, I think the house will fall down.' The young boy looked up at me dubiously.

'Come on, in you come; Francis you get some drinks would you?' I turned to see Carna watching me, a smile on her face. I smiled back feeling relief flood into me.

The children ran through the house like little whirlwinds. I handed out the drinks glad to be doing something as we gathered in the lounge. A rather serious looking Michael came up to me.

'Here you go.' I said handing him a coke.

'Thank you, err...Uncle Francis...' He looked unsure of himself, out of his comfort zone. I knelt down understanding the feeling.

'Yes?'

'Where's your TV?'

'TV....' I repeated a little perplexed.

'Yes, you know television. Theresa and me, we've done a complete turn of the house and no television.'

'You're right, no television.' I looked up at Carna.

'How do you survive?' said my brother wandering over clutching his beer bottle. I realised I had been so wrapped up in my life that television had not entered it.

'We don't have a television.' I stated standing and continuing to look at Carna. She shook her head smiling.

'Do you need one?' She asked. I could see the others watching me, all, I realised, confused now at the lack of television. I shrugged, finding it stranger that I had not even thought about it.

'You need a tele,' said Michael.

'How do you get by of an evening?' My brother chirped up, looking from Carna to myself.

'He's got Carna to keep him busy,' piped in my mother. Rosanna gave a little nervous laugh, looking at the children.

'TV is about escapism, here we like to challenge life head on,' said Carna. They looked at her strangely but did not question it. I gave a grunt of annoyance before I had realised it. She turned and gave me a sad smile. There was a moments silence as they sat mulling over her words. Finally it was broken by Michael.

'What are we going to do?

'Swim, play games.' She said grabbing his hand, 'Come on.'

I felt drained and slightly drunk by the time they all departed at the end of the day. My mother had talked constantly of past events; Pulling out photo albums to help to jog my memory, aunts and uncles, holidays, pictures of me growing up. It was the pictures of a canal boat that cropped up in many of the holiday photos that unnerved me.

'This boat mum, I know it.' I saw her eyes light up, the others turned to look at me expectantly. 'I've seen it in a dream.' I said hesitantly, my eyes drifting to and connecting with those of Carna.

'It's our boat; we holiday on it all the time, you used to come with us when you were young.' She indicated the photos.

'You still have it?' She nodded.

'You borrowed it last year for your holiday, you and Carna.'

'What's its name I can't quite make it out?'

The boat appeared in my dreams throughout the night, sometimes with the family on it sometimes with Carna. I tossed and turned feeling each of them pulling at me.

Each night after that I dreamed, the dream had changed though. I found myself standing on a bridge; on one side stood the family, watching me, on the other stood Carna. I would call out but neither side would answer. I tried to walk toward the family but found that no matter how fast I walked or even ran I was still in the middle, I tried in the other direction, towards Carna with the same result. Before me with a leg on each side of the large canyon that the bridge crossed stood a giant, a two headed god, his beard flowing down over his long toga.

With my sleep so disturbed and broken, within a week I was exhausted and drinking heavily. Carna tried to comfort me; she offered me a relaxing infusion. I remembered the one I had been given earlier in the year and refused.

On the Friday morning she took my hand across the kitchen table 'I thought in the evening we could go down to the Coach and Horses and have a meal. I've booked a table; there's a singer there, I know you like.'

'I like... yes, well I suppose you would know. You know more about me than I do. What if I don't want to go?' I was snappish

'You'll enjoy it, something different, away from the house for an evening. I thought you would relish the chance.' I could not deny that so said no more.

The pub was already busy when we arrived. There was the soft murmuring of conversation and the clatter of plates, knives and forks at the tables. We had come early to eat before the singer started.

'Francis and Carna, good to see you!' Called the barman.

'Hello Paul, We've got a table booked.' Paul nodded and looked across the room.

'Ellie!' he called out. 'Can you show Carna and Francis to their table?' The barmaid who I remembered from my previous visit came over, beaming her arms open as she hugged Carna and kissed me on the cheek.

'Oh I've missed you two, you must come in more often.' She walked us across to a table in a bay window. She chattered incessantly to Carna. I heard the occasional word but zoned out and found my eyes wandering the room, watching the happy groups eating and talking at the tables. I felt Carna nudge me.

'Err sorry?'

'I was saying it should be a good night, he's a good singer, likes doing them ballads, you know.'

'Oh yes right, yep sounds like it should be good.' I muttered sitting down.

'I know what you need Francis, never right till you've had one.' She wandered off and soon returned with a whisky for me and red wine for Carna.

'Here you go that'll sort you out.' She smiled 'I'll come and get your order in a minute.'

As soon as we were settled a stream of visitors came to our table to give their greetings and 'long time no see's'. There were the single men at the bar that I apparently used to discuss fishing and football with. I assured them that my fishing was going swimmingly; my present catch rate making them whistle in surprise.

'Mind always was a lucky bugger,' said an old grey whiskered man. 'beggin yer pardon mam;' he said, quickly apologising to Carna . When they had retired back to the bar a stream of diners got up and came over, well-meaning and friendly all of whom we apparently knew well. The women chatted happily to Carna. The men gravely shook my hand and asked how I was coping since my collapse, all a little unsure as to how to proceed but happy to talk sport and their jobs once I had turned the conversation. Finally we managed to order and our food came.

'Do we really know so many people?' I murmured to Carna. 'I've hardly seen anyone this past ten months.'

'We do now it seems.' She replied smiling; her brilliant blue eyes moist and shining in the firelight. I gave her an enquiring look. 'The game has changed. Now you must meet people.' I looked confused for a while, but she would not say more. I looked into the dancing flames, flickering from the one large log that made the fire. Autumn had arrived and it gave a welcome glow. 'The game...' I thought then remembering Geoff's words, it dawned on me. 'Of course...' I looked back at Carna who smiled sadly.

'Potential candidates...? She nodded in reply.

'Eat your food,' she said pointing at the plates. We ate quietly concentrating on our food; I contemplating the news, she observing me. Finally she said, 'I'm sorry, please don't let it ruin the evening.'

'It's not your fault.' I replied a little bit gruffly. 'The food's good.'

'And the singer is here;' she said quickly. As if on cue a man walked in clutching a guitar. Ellie followed him with a bar stool. I found myself studying the man intently. He looked familiar but I had certainly not come across any singers in the last few months.

'I know him...' I muttered to myself. Carna heard.

'He did well in one of those talent shows on the television a couple of years ago apparently. His picture was regularly in all the magazines then; so Ellie told me anyway. He produced an album and then well...' she tailed off

'So now he's back to pubs and clubs.' I finished absently. I rubbed my forehead and closed my eyes searching for the memory. Suddenly it came. I was in a room, a comfortable lounge, small not like the one in the House, a boy and girl sat on the floor, the girl was singing along to a man, the man, on the television that we were all watching, swinging her arms in time with the music, next to me a woman hummed the tune.

'He's the best.' She said turning and smiling at me. Then they were gone. My head ached, as I opened my eyes. Carna watched me, concern spreading across her face.

'My night out isn't working very well.' She said gently taking my hand. 'He has other ideas it seems.' I saw anger flash in her eyes.

'I saw them…' I spluttered. I did not know how to continue. It was not that easy discussing them with her. Fortunately the man began to play and we turned to listen, unable now to have an easy conversation. I sipped at the beer that I had ordered with my meal. The gentle music, beer and the atmosphere slowly calmed me. I listened keen to hear the singer in the knowledge that I heard him once before.

The words of the chorus floated through the room.

'Sat in the desert waiting to see,
What would happen in the world outside of me.
I swam in the great oceans,
Feeling the suffering of human emotions.
Walked through the ranges,
Feeling the weight of the ages.
I flew through the mountain air,
Feeling my soul laid bare.
I danced in the jungles, full of exuberant life.
I felt its pain, saw its death, felt its strife.'

The words washed over me, heightening the anxiety that I had so nearly squashed. As the song finished and the clapping began, I drank down my beer and stood up. Carna stood too. She had not missed the words and knew how I was feeling. She took my hand and we squeezed through the now crowded bar to the door, finally breaking out into the cool dark night. I breathed deeply, and looked up at the bright clear starlit night.

I turned to her not releasing her hand.

'Sorry, I guess He is getting to me.' She nodded and led me slowly home.

I refused all offers from Carna to go out after that. The doorbell had started to ring regularly as 'friends' came calling to drink coffee and invite us out. I could no longer face anyone and if I heard the door go I sneaked quickly out the back.

By the end of October I was a nervous wreck. I found myself sitting by the remains of an autumn fire in the lounge late one night, an empty bottle of whisky in my hand; in the other I held a knife. Thoughts of ending it all filled my head. I drew it across my arm and watched the rich blood burst to the surface. Amazingly I felt a release of pent up energy as I watched my blood drip onto the pure white rug. Fascinated I watched the blood form drops, the firelight dancing in each one, as they fell slowly to the ground; as they hit the noise seemed to echo around the room, filling my head with a cacophony of sound.

I did not know where the knife had come from. My red blood glistened on its blade. I looked into the burning embers and saw the dancing image of a twofaced head. I was sure it was laughing at me. I swore and threw the knife at it. The fire hissed and crackled. I stood up shakily. Knocking over the coffee table, I staggered across to the wall. My arm rubbed across it, leaving a large blood stain; fascinated I stared at it. It began to form a two faced head. I lurched away from it against the book case my hand upon the dark stone of the Magna Mater. My blood ran down across it I felt a shock of energy surge up my arm. I fell to the floor.

The shimmering image of a woman appeared above me dressed in a long flowing robe, a golden crown upon her head. She reached down and touched the medallion that hung about my neck and smiled. Then she placed a finger on my bleeding arm. I felt it tingle. I tried to move but was unable to. She reached up and put a hand upon my head. With a sigh I instantly dropped into the first deep satisfying sleep I had had in weeks.

No dreams haunted me and when I woke I found myself in my bed. I felt refreshed and with a new idea in my head. I wondered if Cybele had planted it and touched the medallion round my neck. A shiver ran through me. What tricks was she playing I wondered. I had enough problems with a god and a naiad. Carna was not in the room and I could not hear her. I guessed if Cybele had planted the idea in my head then she would make sure Carna was out of the way. I wondered if I should go along with the plan that seemed so formed in my head; was I just playing into their hands, like a chess piece on a board. I wanted out so knew that I would have to give it a try.

I threw back the covers and stood up, stretching, my muscles ached; I realised I had done little exercise for some time apart from the lifting of a whisky tumbler! I remembered the previous evening and looked down at my arm; there was not a mark or blemish on it.

After a shower and some breakfast washed down with a coffee, I began to search the house. I knew that I would find what I was looking for. I just had to look in the right place. It was the nature of the house. I found it in the spare room on top of the wardrobe, a new backpack. I soon had it packed, with some clothes, food and a waterproof sleeping bag which just happened to be with the back pack along with a small camping stove. My wallet was full of money. Walking through the office, I picked up the small notebook, slipping it into an inside pocket then grabbing a full bottle of whisky from the lounge I headed towards the two front doors.

I left the car at the station and walked up to the ticket booth, slowly, as I had not yet decided on a destination. I just knew that I wanted out and needed to leave. It was a small station so I had little choice, south to

London or north to... A city did not seem like a safe option so I decided to go north and get off where-ever there were not many people. I bought a ticket to the furthest northerly destination and went onto the platform. After twenty minutes the small local train chugged into the station with a screech of metal on metal it came to a halt. The automatic doors swung open and I stepped aboard my heart now pounding at the thought of just leaving, running away. The train was soon rattling along the track the carriage almost empty, just an elderly couple sitting at the far end. I settled down and closed my eyes trying to focus my mind and relax. I concentrated on the repeated clunk – clunk as the wheels rolled over the tracks, slowly my pounding heart returned to normal. I felt as though a weight had lifted from my shoulders.

I travelled for the rest of the day and into the night, getting on and off trains, not really caring where they took me. I woke in the morning to the soft tap of rain on the window and the gentle clatter and sway of the carriage. I was alone. Looking out of the window I noticed the rise of mountains in the distance on one side, from the other the sea.

Through my fuzzy thoughts I remembered the last station, large and echoing in the cool of the night, a city, I could not recall its name but there I had made a conscious decision to turn west and head for the mountains, a place buried deep in memory but definitely there, drawing me on.

Finally I stepped out onto the cold grey stone of the platform. A gloomy dawn greeted me. The mountains lay somewhere ahead shrouded in mist. I shivered as the cold damp air seeped instantly through my clothes and into my bones. Lifting my pack upon my back I began to walk, down the waking streets of the small town and out into the countryside, following the road towards the mountains. Cars began to zip past me, as commuters began their journeys, not seeing me in their morning haste. I plodded on; my feet seemed to know where they were going. I just knew that ahead of me lay mountains and behind a world that I could not comprehend, decisions I did not know how to make. Each time I felt their presence I increased my pace, walking with a rhythm, hearing only the footfalls on the country road and the thumping beat of my heart. I focused on them blotting out everything else.

As the day came slowly to an end and light mountain drizzle fell around me, I felt as though I was reaching my destination I had entered a lush valley, a river raged through it. The small country road that I walked weaved along its edge, the granite of the mountain raw at one side, where it had been blasted away in the past. My legs were feeling like jelly, my body ached from the exertions of the day. I felt faint as I had eaten and drunk little.

At a bend in the road ahead I saw them, the two children. They were laughing as they climbed a style over the old wall and began trudging up the farm track that led from the road. Rosie was ahead smiling as they shouted back at me and beckoned me on.

'Come on slow coach!' the night seemed to have disappeared. It was a summer's day, birds called all about me, the river rushed noisily behind. I climbed over the style finding myself shouting,

'I'll beat you to the top.'

'No chance!' said Michael.

'Is it right up there?' Theresa was pointing, with concern at the rugged peak on our left as we walked.

'That's the top of Moel Hebog. It's not on the top but just above the trees there on the ridge.'

'My men are there; they will stop you. I am Owain Glyndwr,' shouted Michael swinging a stick like a sword in front of me.

'In that case I must be Henry 1V coming to track you down. I will have Wales under my control.' I shouted and laughing picked up a stick. 'Charge!' soon we were trading sword blows.

'Stop, you two before someone gets hurt!' called Rosie. I allowed Michael to give me a gentle hit and collapsed to the ground.

'Arr! You have got me you brigand, all is lost.'

'I am victorious!' he shouted raising his sword in the air. Now I will take you as a prisoner to my mountain cave.'

I felt myself as an observer in my own body. We marched on across the meadow and into the woods beyond. I felt Rosie take my hand and my heart raced as I studied her smile.

'Here's the turn' I heard myself say. A footpath sign pointed up into the pine woods alongside a mountain stream. The track weaved its way up steeply through the dappled shade and hues of green, the air cool. Water rushed down beside us amongst moss and fern clad rocks. It was a magical trail, which added to my strange situation as an observer. The family trudged upward puffing. I soon found myself pulling Michael up, his sword now a walking stick, as Rosie helped Theresa. We stopped regularly.

As we sat eating snacks and drinking in a small glade by the stream, I found myself not wanting to reach the top as feelings of endearment and connection to this family overwhelmed me. Time seemed to have no meaning. I was not aware of how long we walked or played in the woods or stream.

Of a sudden we burst out of the trees and onto the lower reaches of the ridge. The sunlight beat down on us.

'Where is it Dad?' Said Michael, his face was red with heat and exhaustion, but there was a light in his eyes. 'Where's his cave.' He lifted his walking stick and waved it as it once again became his sword.

'Up to the right over there, see where the rock face is.' I pointed.

'I think so.' He said uncertainly. 'Nobody would have found him up here.'

'No that's why he did so well against Henry. He could retreat up here and then keep rushing down to attack and harass the English army. We scrambled across the upland heath and rocks until the opening of the cave became clear.

'I see it.' shouted Michael and was off at a run.

'He'll sleep well tonight,' said Rosie, coming up beside me still pulling Theresa along.

The cave was large and disappeared back into darkness. Michael had gone in and I could hear him whooping and shouting. We turned and looked out across the woodland below. Snowdon loomed across the valley. A small village nestled in a junction between three valleys below us two rivers met there and flowed on down the third valley.

'Is that where we are staying? It seems so small,' said Theresa.

'It is and it does, doesn't it. Look over there you can see the little steam train coming along the valley; look at the line of smoke coming from the engine.'

'Are you coming in!' shouted Michael. 'It's damp in here and rocky. I can't imagine sleeping up here. It would be a bit uncomfortable.'

'And a bit scary,' said Theresa. We turned and walked in.

It went dark and I found myself being pulled away. I knew I was leaving them and felt the emotional wrench. In my heart I did not want to go.

I woke groggily, feeling cold and damp through. I felt my body shivering on the wet cold grey granite. My muscles ached. I was disorientated as I pulled myself up into a sitting position.

Looking around I realised that I was in a cave. Not just any cave it was the cave, Owain Glyndwr's cave on the side of Moel Hebog in Snowdonia, Wales. Mist hung at the entrance obscuring the view but I recognised the spot and I realised it was not just from the vision that I had seemed to live in which had brought me here, but also from my memory. It was there, the cave, the holiday with my family. I remembered them now. I realised that I remembered everything. It had come back to me.

My body shook now from emotion, I felt tears stream down my weather beaten cheeks and into the stubble on my chin. Memories flooded through me like an old cine film, holidays, the children, their births, my marriage, my youth. I pulled the medallion out of my shirt and placed it between my fingers. I felt a warm glow come from it. I felt strength enter me.

'Cybele...' I whispered quietly into the wind. I knew it was her. She had done this, brought me here and returned my memory. The mist blew clear, revealing a rugged autumn mountain scene. Grey clouds scudded across the valley below blotting out the peaks opposite.

The wildness about me emanated with strength and power. For a moment the sun shone, then just as quickly it was blotted out and rain clouds blew in. I stood at the entrance of the cave watching the wave of rain sweep up the valley and over the trees finally splashing down in front of me like a beaded curtain. I stepped back, shivering again. The clouds grumbled with thunder. Janus was not happy.

Retreating to my backpack I pulled out my camping stove and cooked up some food and hot tea, which I ate sitting in my sleeping bag watching the rain. He did not need to worry. I was now even more confused. I wanted to return of that I was sure, but how could I put anyone into this turmoil and even if I could who would I choose?

I slumped back against the cold granite and wondered if Owain Glyndwr had leaned there, looking out, wondering at his future. I remembered that in 1408 he had disappeared. I wondered what had happened to him and guessed that Carna was most likely involved. The thought allowed a wry smile to creep into my face. It did not last long as I wondered what I should do now.

I stayed, routed by my dilemma for a few days. It had rained constantly, but on the morning of the fourth day, grey clouds hung high in a crisp cold air. My food had run out and I knew that I had to leave the cold security of the cave. The world outside was calling again. The game had not let me go just yet; I knew I would have to play it until the end. I wondered if that would be my own as I packed up my meagre belongings and walked down into the trees.

XII

November disappeared in a cold slightly drunken haze as I wandered from village to town and then back to the countryside of Wales and West England, drinking heavily every time I found myself thinking of a solution. Slowly I gravitated towards London. My money ran out and when I tried my bank card I found that it would not work. I knew Janus was forcing my hand.

I was cold and dirty. I had not washed for over a week I had not shaved for a month and possessed quite a beard. My clothes were torn and wearing thin from the constant wear and tear. I sat on a bench and looked across at the station. I had enough left for a ticket to London, or of course I could drink it away and be damned.

I wondered why I thought of London and yet it seemed the natural place for lost souls to gravitate to. Picking up my bag I bought a ticket and boarded the next train. No one sat near me, which I did not mind. It had been some weeks since I had been self-conscious about my odour or looks. I relished the warmth that caused a steam to rise out of my damp clothing, and settled down to sleep through my journey.

London did not give me answers, just more problems; I wandered the streets in a daze. Without realising it I had slowly found my way to a small park by the Thames River. It felt familiar. My senses suddenly became alert. I could feel her presence close by- Carna. My skin tingled, I felt sweat on my brow. I looked around. I remembered my last visit to London to see Geoff. The garden I was in no longer had the beautiful scented flower beds they were now laid bare with cold dun coloured earth.

I recognised the small bridge off to one side and quickly walked up onto it. It spanned a small road but I did not look down my view was drawn to the large mansion in the distance. I knew they were not far away. I did not want to visit them but felt drawn. I turned, my feet dragging as I retraced my steps off the bridge and turned onto the winter lawn. A flock of jackdaws, beaks pecking amongst the blades of grass, flew up in annoyance at my arrival. I did not want to look up but trudged across the lawns feeling the dark, now menacing yew hedge enclosing me on each side. The sound of water grew louder at my approach, a cold noise in the grey dusk. Finally my feet left the grass and joined the path surrounding the fountain and I looked up. There they were the seven Naiads, white and distant now. I remembered their warmth and beauty before on that summer's afternoon. Now Venus looked upon me with a cold marble calculating gaze. I shivered involuntarily and my eyes filled with uncontrollable tears. I collapsed down in front of the statue and let my emotions break free. When I finally became conscious of where I was it was dark and cold, the air was damp and full of moisture. I pulled out my sleeping bag, moved over to a small gate in the wall and curled up, falling into a fitful shivery sleep.

Suddenly I felt a pain in my side. I groaned and rolled over opening my eyes. I was staring at some trainers, scuffed and worn. I rolled over and found myself looking up at a group of youths, who were all leering at me. I sat up feeling the pain in my side.

They were shouting at each other and laughing, through the haze that filled my head I could not work out what they were saying. One of them grabbed the end of my sleeping bag and pulled it off me. The next minute it was a flaming torch. I felt the heat of it. They danced around it like fiends, their shadows from the flames dancing on the surrounding walls.

One of them came over and poured a can of lager over my head the others laughed pulling my backpack from me and emptying out my belongings onto the floor. I stood up in protest and received a punch in the face. Dazed I staggered backwards into the doorway. I felt a kick in my stomach. The air burst out of my lungs. Kicks and blows rained down on me. I felt myself vomit. It made them jump away from me. I wiped blood from my nose. The noise of them filled my ears, my vision was blurred. I was afraid and felt the adrenalin pump through my body.

They threw the remainder of my belongings onto the fire and then wandered away laughing. It was then that the tears came, trickling slowly down my cheeks, mixing with my blood and vomit. As I watched my belongings burn I reached into my inside pocket and gave a sigh of relief as I touched the battered notebook.

I felt a sudden warmth at my chest and pulled out the medallion, clutching it close, I felt the pain ease and fell into a dream ridden sleep of gods and goddesses, my family, Carna and her parade of men.

I woke hungry and thirsty. How had I reached such a low point? I crawled over to a park bench in front of the fountain and its statues. I felt their empty eyes upon me. I lay down on the bench pulling my knees up, trying to alleviate some of the pain. Time blurred and before I knew it night was falling again. I did not have the energy to move and felt the December frost creep through my clothes. My will was slipping away. I could not see the point any longer. As I fell into a fitful sleep I prayed that I would not wake up.

I did of course but it was not the morning. I was woken by someone shaking my shoulder. All was hazy and they seemed far away. I felt warm where I was and knew that they were stopping me from slipping quietly away. I felt annoyed that even now I could not escape. I did not want to wake. They were insistent constantly shaking me and rubbing my limbs. Finally I gave in and returned groaning and trying to focus on them.

'Hello mate; thought we had lost you there.' I felt myself being lifted up. 'Just going to put you in the ambulance; take you to the hospital; get you tidied up a bit ok.' I grunted, too weak to have any choice in the matter. I felt the ambulance bumping along the road.

'Why?'

'Why, what?' came the distant reply from the man in green who peered down at me.

'Why didn't you just leave me? I was warm, comfortable; in a good place, no one bothering me.' I mumbled weakly.

'You can't escape that easily,' came the reply. His voice sounded different, deeper. I grabbed his arm and tried to focus. His face I was sure it was different, blurred as though another looked through him a face with a beard, a face I knew; a face on a face- two!

'No' I shouted hoarsely, 'Get away' I tried feebly to push him away but I had no strength.

'Relax Mister; we are just taking you in to the hospital. I felt some straps come over my body, restraining my arms. I felt an injection in my arms. I felt calmer and slipped off into restful sleep.

I came round in the hospital, lying on a hard mattress under a crisp clean sheet and blanket. My skin tingled with cleanliness. I was wearing a hospital gown and had a drip in my arm. The cage-like sides of my bed were up. My eyes slowly scanned the ward, taking in the four patients opposite and those to the left of me. I was on the end, the nurse station near me. A nurse noticed my movement and called to a male nurse who quickly came across to me.

'Hello sir, how are you feeling?'

'Rotten' I croaked.

'Here let me get you some water.' He moved across to the bedside to get me some water; his eyes not leaving me. I noticed the other nurse also watching nervously. 'Here.' I took the plastic cup and drank, spilling as much as I managed to swallow through my swollen throat. 'You've had a bit of a beating. We've patched you up a bit.' I mumbled a thank you. A movement caught my eye and a uniformed security guard appeared. 'The ambulance man said you were a bit aggressive when they picked you up. We weren't sure how you would respond when you woke.' The nurse said by way of explanation. He smiled still looking wary and not coming to close.

I lay back and looked up at the white ceiling, trying to gather my thoughts. Slowly I became aware of the aches and pains that seemed to cover virtually all of my body.

'Could you tell us your name sir? We can contact your family then if you would like us to?' I saw two smiling children and my wife looking down at me. The vision faded, to be replaced by another of Carna at her most stunning, behind her towered the huge two faced Janus and the flowing figure of Cybele, whose smile seemed to tear at my soul.

'Name?' I croaked.

'Yes sir.' The man had stepped a little closer and looked down at me. He was young, strong; his dark hair was gelled up. His deep brown eyes watched me.

'No name.' I said closing my eyes, not wanting Carna to claim me just yet. I did not speak again that day, refusing the nurses entreaties. I ate hungrily at meal times feeling my strength slowly return.

That night I fell into a restless sleep, dreaming of my family. I felt them close to me as though they were living flesh. I ran my hands through Rosie's soft brown hair. I felt the texture of her lips on mine. I could smell her perfume, I lifted my laughing children, spinning them round and feeling the weight of them through my biceps. My dream abruptly changed to Carna; Her supple body swimming naked across the pool, smiling back at me, beckoning me to join her. I sat up suddenly awake, it was dark and warm in the hospital ward, I sensed other patients around me in restless slumber, a movement drew my eye to the nurses station. The young nurse on duty had looked up and was watching me, concern in her eyes. I looked away my hand suddenly clutching the medallion at my neck. It calmed me. I felt a warm presence sweep over me.

'Are you all right sir?' the nurse was standing at the bottom of the bed. I nodded absently and lay down. She breathed out in relief and turned away. Holding the medallion I dropped into a deep sleep.

When I woke the medallion was still in my hands, warm and glistening as I looked at it. I felt calm; calmer than I had felt in a long time.

'Good morning.' a spectacled face came into focus looking down at me. Dark rimmed spectacles over watery blue eyes, a high lined forehead, no hair apart from a rim of grey, the nose was smooth and finely carved, out of character with the rest. The thin mouth held a slight smile. 'My name is Marcus Pickles.' I pulled myself up. The man sat down; watching me closely. I did not speak but it did not faze him. Taking his glasses off and pulling a handkerchief from his pocket he proceeded to clean them; his watery eyes still watching me intently. 'I am a doctor, the hospital psychiatrist to be precise.' He paused studying my reaction. 'I see that this does not worry you or surprise you. I also see that you understand.' He replaced his spectacles. 'Perhaps you could help me by answering a few questions.' It was a statement as though he expected nothing else but my cooperation. I nodded automatically; then felt angry that I had given in so easily. He did not smile at his success with my quick acquiescence but blurted out his first question.

'Could you tell me what happened at the park?' I tried to reply but my mouth was dry and my lips bruised and swollen. He passed me some water and I drank greedily not realising how thirsty I was.

'Youths,' I spluttered between mouthfuls. The water dribbled down my chin.

'Ah, that's what the police thought. Your belongings had all been burned. You have taken quite a beating but you will recover. No broken bones, just lots of nasty bruising apparently.' I nodded, He sat silent for a moment, trying to draw more from me but I just watched him.

'It's a nice park that. I love those statues.' His change of direction caught me off guard.

'Why?' I blurted. I saw his surprise.

'Err, I suppose they represent beauty, spirituality, nature…. immortality. Do you not like them?'

'I have seen the life they came from.' He looked at me bemused but said nothing, wanting me to continue. I could not stop myself. 'They are what you say but they are also power, control, manipulation. They can take you to heaven and lead you to your doom.' I slumped back in the pillows closing my eyes. He was silent for a moment digesting my words. Then he coughed slightly to get my attention. I looked across at him. He was studying my face. My stare did not put him off.

'Tell me; what do you mean by your phrase 'I have seen the life they came from'?' I closed my eyes again.

'Statues have to come from somewhere, a thought, a vision a picture of perceived reality.'

'Ah I see you know their background, their development so to speak.'

'You could say that.'

'I think they have meaning to you beyond what others see.' He said perceptively, 'It is why you were there?' I nodded my head vaguely.

'I guess so.' A trolley arrived in the middle of the ward.

'Tea, coffee,' called the assistant. Our moment was broken. I felt thirst and hunger take over. Dr Pickles stood.

'Tea' I croaked as loud as I could.

'I'll come back later if that's ok.' It was not a question so I smiled.

'How long will they keep me?'

'It's not a prison.' He smiled back.

'No but they will want the bed.'

'I'll not let them throw you out just yet.' He said leaving. 'I want to know why those statues mean what they mean to you.' I took my tea and a biscuit. When I looked up he had disappeared. I mulled over our conversation through the day as I studied the comings and goings in the ward. It was good just to sit and watch and not to care or worry for a while. For this short while there was no expectation. I did not have to speak listen or do anything.

At first, as I thought about Dr Pickles I did not fancy continuing our conversation, but as the day went on I found myself thinking about what I could say to him, possible conversations ran through my head. By the end of the day I was looking out for him and expecting his arrival. I felt frustrated that he did not come back and felt certain that he was playing me.

When he finally arrived late morning the next day I was keen to talk.

'Good morning err…, 'he looked down at my chart. 'Ah still no name I see.'

'May be later, names can cause problems.' He nodded understanding and sat down next to the bed.

'You look better.'

'Yes I'm feeling much better thank you.' Even after all the time I had had to think of our conversation I realised that I had not come to a decisive plan as to how it should go.

'So…' he took off his glasses, pulled out his handkerchief and began to rub the lenses. 'Those statues…'

'If I tell you my story, you will diagnose me as schizophrenic and prescribe me some medication.'

'Are you?'

'I don't think so.' He stopped rubbing the lens and looked at me.

'Have you had medication before?' I shook my head, 'Previous discussions were leading you down that route though?' I nodded. He lent back in his chair and carefully replaced his glasses. 'So the questions we need to get to the bottom of are: Why do you think I will diagnose you as schizophrenic and why you don't think you are?'

'I don't have to discuss it with you.'

'No you don't but I think you have reached an impasse. You need a way of moving on.' He looked out of the window watching the dust dance in the sunbeams that broke through, giving me a chance to consider.

'The thing is…' I paused to gather my thoughts and took a deep breath. I knew that he was correct and I needed to find a way. 'I see before me two realities.' He looked up, his eyes sparkled with interest. 'I have studied them both and come to the conclusion that they are in fact real. This I know you will never accept, which is why you will diagnose me as schizophrenic.' I paused again, studying his face watching his reactions. 'But to me they are undoubtedly real and I must choose between them. The difficulty is that in their separate ways they both offer exactly what I have always wanted. They reach to both ends of my personality.' His face studied me intently. I knew that he was keen to hear more. I could see that he dare not move. He did not speak he did not want to interrupt me. I looked down at my hands resting on the bed covers. 'You see I have ended up running away from both possibilities. In my indecision and fear of getting it wrong I have….' I was unsure how to continue. He finished for me.

'You have ended up here.'

'Yes' I grunted back.

'I see that you have done all the diagnosing for me so is there any chance that you could tell me about these two realities?'

'I don't know' I studied his face; the lined forehead was creased in concentration as he watched me. 'I don't want you locking me up.' I finished lamely for in truth I really did not know how to go about telling him.

He chuckled and leant back in his chair.

'We don't do that if we can help it. Not the best way to treat someone you know.' We were disturbed once again by the tea trolley. This time Dr Pickles had a tea with me and we sat silently together watching the others on the ward being served while we drank. A decorative streamer in the window fluttered down and a nurse helping at the tea trolley went across to fix it back up.

'Christmas is coming.' He watched me once again looking for reaction. I realised with some shock that I had not even taken note of the few streamers and the faded green Christmas bell that hung across the window. I realised that the nurses' station was similarly decorated and a small Christmas tree sat on a table in the corner. He noted my surprise. 'You had not realised.'

I shook my head and muttered, 'When?'

'It's the 22nd today, so in three days.'

'Three days.' My mind went into free fall as I grasped with this concept. 'I ...' I just shook my head, months had gone by whilst I wandered, it had seemed like days, but I knew I had left the house in October. My hand subconsciously reached up and grasped the medallion. I felt its calming effect. I felt the presence of the Magna Mater watching me, willing me on; reminding me that I had to make a decision. I could not keep running away.

'The Medallion...?' I refocused on Dr Pickles and saw his eyes upon my hand around the medallion.

'It's nothing.' I mumbled.

'No, it is. What is on it? Can I see?' I did not want him to look, but he was already leaning forward, reaching out. I let go of it and he lifted it up from my chest leaning close he concentrated. I stared at his forehead, shiny and pale in the florescent lighting.

'A head, woman's head wearing a crown; There is some writing around it;' his muffled voice said into my chest. I felt him flip the coin over. 'A box with something in; can't quite make it out.' He suddenly looked up, surprising me. I jerked back against the pillows, my hand subconsciously checking that the medallion still hung around my neck on its leather thong. 'Looks old, but somehow new; I'm guessing silver.' His inquisitive gaze returned to my face. 'Intriguing; what does the writing say?'

'Magna Mater.' I replied reflexively before I could stop myself.

'Ah, the mother of the gods;' He sat back in his chair.

'The Earth Mother, The Mother Goddess, the Great Mother, Cybele' I mumbled.

'Yes indeed; is she important to you?' he paused then as an afterthought said, 'like the statues?' I nodded. 'Is she part of one of your realities?' I nodded again watching him carefully, trying to gauge his thoughts. I decided to test him

'Do you think the gods existed?'

'You mean the ancient gods of Greece and Rome?' I nodded again, staying silent, wanting him to continue. 'I was fascinated with them in my youth when I studied the Classics.' I could see he did not want to answer.

'But did they exist?'

'Well' he said cautiously. 'We know them only from stories, ancient texts.' He stared up at the light, as it hummed and flickered; 'Although, the same could be said of our current faiths.' He thought for a moment. 'I could not categorically deny that they existed although personally I don't think so.' He said looking directly at me, his eyes large behind his glasses, twinkled, expectantly.

'A year ago I don't think I would have given it a second thought.' I said. 'Although to be honest I could not be sure.'

'How so?'

'Something happened … then I had an accident, lost my memory.'

'When you say something happened – what do you mean?' I smiled at him.

'Apparently I walked into another reality; Left my old life behind.'

'So this is the other reality?'

'Yes.'

'Do the gods exist here or in your old reality?'

'Here.'

'Gosh.' We sat silent for a while both unsure of the next step. Dr Pickles finally moved in his chair. 'Are you able to show me?'

I realised suddenly that I had been given a way but could I? Did I want to? The medallion felt warm, I realised I was still clutching it in my hand. I felt Cybele's influence.

'Maybe I could,' I found myself saying, 'although you must be sure.' I closed my eyes and lay back in the pillows. 'There is no going back.' I muttered. I could not face him.

'No going back' I heard him say. There was lightness in his voice. I knew he did not believe.

I open my eyes sat up and swung my legs off the bed, facing him. He pulled himself back in the chair, unsure of what to expect. My head reeled with dizziness. I felt movement at the nurses station and sensed them rising and moving towards me.

'Think on it. If you really want to find out, to see them, to give up what you have in this life, then visit me tomorrow, if you decide that you do not, then don't come back.' I breathed out releasing the pressure within me. Now I was committed. Before the nurses could reach us I swung my legs back on the bed rolled over and closed my eyes, moaning at the pains the sudden movement had caused me. I felt them around me, looking uncertain. I heard the chair move back and Dr Pickles stand up.

'Everything o.k. Dr Pickles,' the nurse said.

'Yes…Yes, fine thank you nurse. I think…' I sensed him remove his glasses and a handkerchief from his pocket. He slowly wiped the lenses. 'I think we are done here for today. Err good-bye Mr … err.'

'Francis' I said not turning.

'Thank you. Good bye Francis.'

I spent much of the rest of the day dozing, thinking on nothing. If thoughts entered my head I quickly grabbed the medallion which gave me a warm sense of calm and peace. I did not want to think about anything. I had decided to let Dr Pickles make the decisions. If he came back I would challenge him. It would be his choice to agree or not. He would choose my reality through his decisions.

He turned up in the late afternoon on the following day. My rest had made me feel much better. The bruises ached but I was feeling strong and healing quickly. I was sitting up when he appeared. I had half hoped that he would not.

'Good morning Francis.'

'Dr Pickles'

'Marcus, please.'

'Marcus' He nodded and sat down.

'Warm in here today' He pulled out his handkerchief mopped his brow and proceeded to rub the lenses of his glasses.

'So you came back.'

'You are my patient. I have to see you. Besides why would I not want you to show me the gods?' I knew he spoke metaphorically.

'Because, to meet the gods, you too will have to discover another self, another reality. Your world will change irrevocably. You will be faced with decisions and dilemmas that currently you cannot even perceive.' He looked perplexed by my statement.

'That is indeed strong. But is it not my job, my path in life, to follow these leads that are thrown to me. To discover what affects the human mind, how it does so and why.'

'You see me as a patient, mentally ill, deceived by my own mind.' Suddenly I felt doubt, could this be so? I decided that there was only one way to find out. I could see he was unsure how to respond for once.

'Each of us is different. Our minds, thoughts, take us all in different directions. Which is the right path? Who knows? There is of course the accepted comfortable route that society can cope with. Anybody outside of that will soon be labelled. I try not to see people as patients or mentally ill. Rather as those individuals who are exploring different routes to the expected norm.'

'So where do you see yourself?' I probed. He looked up and studied the light. A habit he had when he was looking inward rather than delving into my thoughts.

'I suppose I can fit in to the accepted norm. At least most people see me that way but underneath I feel there is more that I don't understand. That tantalises me but lies just out of my reach, but affects me all the same leaving me a little unsure. I guess that is what drove me to become a psychiatrist. To see if I could find answers through the minds of others.'

'So how brave are you? How far would you go in your exploration?' He rubbed his chin thoughtfully, absentmindedly taking off his glasses, and reaching into his pocket for his handkerchief, then he changed his mind and replaced them.

'I would like to think that I would be prepared to reach out far enough to discover new thoughts and ideas …directions that we should go perhaps.' I was about to ask another question when he held up his hand. 'You are taking over; surely it is my turn for some questions, after all that is what I am paid for.' He smiled.

'Just one more.'

'Ok then.'

'You do not wear a ring, are you married? Do you have any children' He fidgeted, uncomfortable.

'That is a bit off piste isn't it? I am not supposed to discuss my personal life.' I became a little irritable.

'I did not ask you here. You do not have to stay. You came back.' I folded my arms and turned to watch the patient opposite who was trying unsuccessfully to get the attention of the nurse at the desk.

'Ok, I cannot see that it will do any harm.' I turned to him expectantly. 'My wife left me some years ago; said I kept analysing her.' He smiled sadly. 'I have a daughter at college.' I nodded. My stomach churned; a daughter, although some ties were needed I was sure of that.

'My turn now; are you able to show me the gods that haunt you?' The word haunt seemed to echo through me. Perhaps that was how it was.

'Ok.' I replied firmly. 'New Year's Eve. Will you come with me on New Year's Eve?'

'Where to?'

'My house.' He deliberated on my words.

'I should not. I…'

'You do not trust me?' I saw his uncertainty. Before he could answer I continued. 'You will come to no physical harm from me I promise you that. If you come to my house then you will know.' He sat back in his chair watching me.

'I guess I must come alone.' I nodded, my gaze intent. 'You are a strange one. Different; I can't quite fathom it. My professional diagnosis as you well know is that you are schizophrenic.' He paused, this time taking off his glasses and beginning to clean them. I felt as though we were in a bubble the rest of the ward seemed fuzzy and quiet not part of us. 'Although… I don't know there is something more I perceive.' I could see he wanted to. Suddenly he put on his glasses. 'This is nonsense.' He murmured to himself. Then said 'I should not, no cannot, go with you. The hospital would not allow it.' I deliberated on his answer, feeling deflated. It was as though my last hopes had faded. I touched the medallion.

'How about you bring someone? They would have to sit in the car while you come to the door though.' I dare not look at him; instead I focused on my hands as they twisted the sheet into a knot. His chair scraped back and he stood and stretched. There was an unnatural tension in our bubble and he was feeling it to.

'I'll think on it. New Year's Eve you say. Ok, I'll think on it. If I can bring someone then maybe it's possible. It will certainly help us establish who you are and get you settled back at home and for that reason the hospital may allow it.'

'Can I stay here till then?'

'You may have to move wards but we will keep you until then.' I looked up at him. The bubble had burst; the noise of the ward now invaded us. Dinner was being brought round. My body responded to his answer with a wave of endorphins. I lay back and smiled. 'Good bye Francis. Have a good Christmas.'

I was placed into what I assumed was a psychiatric ward the next day, Christmas eve. The noise of the patients and constant comings and goings of staff kept me awake so that I was morose and agitated throughout Christmas Day. I did my best to pretend it was not happening. I managed to get a visit to the small hospital library, but was scared to pick out a book as my choice may be influenced. Finally I took a fictional story about a Sicilian detective; Nothing to do with the mystical world that I could see. So with the curtains pulled round my bed space, ear plugs in, I read my way through Christmas. The intervening days that followed I filled with a jigsaw, television and further books about the Sicilian detective, who appeared to roll through life in a rather casual and haphazard way, always solving the crime.

On the night of the 30th I slept little; feelings of guilt and anticipation overwhelmed me. I had not heard or seen Dr Pickles and had been told that he was on leave until after the New Year which had perplexed me. Now feeling fit and healthy, I spent New Year's day morning pacing up and down the ward and the attached corridors at the end of which I came across locked doors. The nurses left me alone and let me pace. I had refused breakfast and also lunch, just drank mug after mug of tea. Finally my agitation overcame me and I approached the nurses' desk.

'Dr Pickles said he would see me today; is he coming?'

'I think he is on holiday.' said the young nurse. She yawned and looked up unenthusiastically. She looked tired, too many late nights through the festive season, I guessed.

'Can you ring him and check? It's just he said...' she shook her head.

'I couldn't do that. If he's on holiday he would not be happy with me.' I banged the desk making her jump.

'He told me he would come.'

'He probably got the days muddled. He'll be here in a couple of days.'

'No!' I shouted, 'That's too late. He said he would be here.' The nurse, now worried had stood up and took a pace away from the desk. A figure appeared at the office door, another male nurse was already moving towards me along the corridor yet another was moving up through the ward. They were experienced with agitated patients on this ward I had discovered over the last few days and did not want to become their next problem so I took a few deep breaths. The senior nurse standing at the office gave me a severe look.

'What's the problem Francis?' I felt like a child who had tantrumed. I stayed quiet for a moment letting my heart rate drop, sensing the two male nurses closing in on me from each side.

'I do apologise for disturbing you.' I said finally, 'but Dr Pickles said he would see me today.' She gave me another stern look over her steel rimmed glasses.

'I'll have a look.' She disappeared into the office. The three other nurses now stood motionless around me waiting. I nodded and smiled at them.

I could hear a rustling of papers; she was taking her time. I began to drum my fingers on the desk impatiently, making the nurse nervous. Finally she came out shaking her head.

'No doesn't look as though he was expecting to come in.' she looked up at me. I could see she was trying to gauge how I was taking this information. 'At least I cannot find any note of it. That does not mean to say that he won't...' She looked over my shoulder. 'Arr... talk of the devil.' I turned to see Dr Pickles coming down the corridor. I felt the nurses all breathe out a collective sigh of relief. 'Dr Pickles, Francis here was just asking...'

'Just arrived in time I think.' He said taking in the situation immediately. 'I do apologise I forgot to write it on the notes that I was coming. Francis and I are going on a trip.'

'But...' I could see the senior nurse's concern.

'Don't worry Sister. I have organised for Michael to come along. He's waiting with the car.'

'Michael?' I said enquiring before the nurse could reply. Dr Pickles turned and smiled.

'He's one of the nurses Francis.' He turned to look at the senior nurse. I followed his gaze. I could see she was not happy.

'You'll have to sign some papers.' She said gruffly. Dr Pickles smiled sweetly to her.

'Of course, Sister.' He turned and looked at me. 'I can see you are going to need a moment to get ready. I'll sign the papers while you sort yourself out.' I was standing in hospital pyjamas, bare feet and with a good growth on my face. I rubbed my chin and nodded.

The clothes I had arrived in had been laundered but they were in a poor state. Some of the more ingrained blood and dirt marks had not come out. The tears had not been repaired. I washed and shaved quickly and pulled them on; checked that I had my medallion and my notebook. I did not have anything else to pack so with one last look at the bed space that had been my resting place for the last week and a half I nodded to the nurses and followed Dr Pickles down the corridor. Dr Pickles used his Identity card to open the door. Soon we were outside and into the cold air. I shivered as a few snowflakes drifted down. Not enough to settle but it reminded you that temperatures were down to freezing. Dusk was already closing in; the heavy low clouds quickly darkening.

'Car's over there. I invited Michael; hope you don't mind. You did say I could bring somebody.' I remembered him mentioning the nurse. 'Thought I had better stick to procedure.' My mind whirled around the possible implications that the nurse would pose.

'No, not a problem.' I folded my arms, trying to keep warm as we made our way across to the car. Dr Pickles hesitated at the door and looked at me a little embarrassed.

'You had better sit in the back with Michael. Once again, I hope you don't mind.' I nodded and opened the back door and sat down. Michael grabbed my hand and shook it. He was a big blonde bear of a man, late twenties I guessed. He smiled.

'Just along for the ride, you know how it is.' I nodded my acceptance. Dr Pickles, got into the driver's seat and looked over his shoulder at me.

'Right Francis, Where are we to go?' I named the town. Dr Pickles and Michael gave a sharp intake of breath. 'I thought you were local. That's an hour and a half's drive. I'm not sure...' He looked at Michael, who looked down at his watch. There was an awkward silence as they both tried to decide what to do. I let out a sigh. I had forgotten how far from home I was. I felt the moment slip through my grip. I pushed open the car door and began to get out.

'How long will you need there professor?' Michael said. I turned to watch them both. Dr Pickle's looked at me enquiringly. A snow flake drifted down and landed on my cheek. I felt it melting.

'Half an hour?'

'About three and a half hours in total then and back here for around...' he looked at his watch, 'seven thirty... eight at the latest. That's good for me. A bit of over-time and still time to get out and party the year away.' He smiled at us both. I looked at Dr Pickles expectantly, still only half in the car. He made up his mind.

'Ok let's give it a go then. Get in Francis. Michael can you set this sat nav. I'm useless with this technology.' I clambered in quickly and slammed the door shutting out the cold. The car was already moving. Michael and Dr Pickles both tried to get me to talk during the journey, but I huddled in the corner and remained stubbornly silent. They chatted to each other for a while and then put on some music. The journey was agonisingly slow. I spent the time wondering what I would find on reaching the House and playing out in my mind what might happen. Eventually we reached the town and I became more alert as the adrenalin flowed through me. I sat up and directed them through the town centre and out into the suburbs, finally we turned into the cul-de-sac and I nervously looked across at the House. It was as I had remembered. The two large doors like giant empty eyes stared out at me. I felt myself shake nervously.

'Nice round here.' Michael said. 'Which one is yours?' I pointed not trusting myself to speak. 'Wow that's one hell of a home.' I force a smile, feeling Dr Pickle's eyes upon me. We pulled up onto the drive in front of the house. The street seemed quiet, the air somehow heavy; the street lamps creating small cones of light, through a freezing mist. They both looked at the large house and back at me. Shadows, from the branches of the trees on the lawn, like long gnarled fingers, moved across the grass and over the car. I felt an involuntary shiver run through me at the same time I was sure I was sweating profusely.

'Why two doors?' Dr Pickles enquired. I shrugged; then tried to speak but my throat was too dry.

'Want me to come in?' Said Michael; Dr Pickles shook his head.

'No I should be ok. Give me five minutes at any rate. I'll give you the thumbs up.' He nodded. 'Come on then Francis, let's go then.' We climbed out of the car. The oppressive cold enveloped us. I pulled my threadbare jumper around me and leaning forward, headed for the house. I could not look at Dr Pickles who followed behind. I felt him stop just before we reached the doors and I turned nervously. He was studying the great doors.

'Impressive, they look ancient. The door knockers…, two heads, they look like one of the gods.' He turned to me enquiringly.

'Janus.' I could feel his mind whirring trying to drag up memories of the gods from his classical education. I did not want him to dwell. 'A roman god,' I studied him nervously, my heart pounding, 'God of beginnings, transitions and endings.'

'Fits with a doorway.' He watched me intently through the mist. 'Part of your realities? Is he real?' I nodded. 'Mm, I am not sure I want to meet him.'

'You won't' I said hurriedly concerned that he would back away. I had come too far now. I had to follow this through to its conclusion. He smiled at me.

'You are concerned about this, coming back here.' I looked enquiringly. 'Your nervousness is written all over your face. Who lives here?' There was tension in his question.

'Just my wife,' I mumbled.

'No dangerous gods then.' I shook my head. 'Do I need Michael?' I could feel his eyes boring into me. I shook my head again and tried to smile confidently. I felt his indecision, so moved quickly to the left hand door.

'Come on, let's go in;' on reaching the door I realised that I did not have a key. I lifted the door knocker the vast ring that hung from Janus, like a giant torch; it felt heavy. The noise was muffled by the fog but the door began to swing open immediately, before anyone could have reached it. Carna stood in the corridor. Her beauty shone, enveloping me and pushing back the crushing dark. I felt my-self bound to her; pulled towards her. I rushed forward into the house. How could I have ever thought of leaving her? My mind thrashed in turmoil. When I reached her, I became unsure; she took my hands and smiling kissed me on the cheek.

'Hello Francis.' Her eyes bore into me. 'You have bought someone with you.' There was sadness in her voice. I nodded; for a moment I had forgotten that I had not returned alone; the hospital, the journey, it had all evaporated. She had stepped back and released my hands.

Offhandedly she said 'He will do.' Her attention now moved to the door. It was as if the temperature around me had suddenly dropped and the lights dimmed.

'Hello Marcus.' Her eyes glistened as she focused on him. Dr Pickles had removed his glasses as they had steamed up with the warmth of the hall. He squinted at her. I wondered what he saw as I pulled my coat around myself and shivered.

'Ah Hello, um, you know my name?'

'Of course I do. How could I not?' she turned to me, her eyes cold and icy blue. 'Now is your time if you wish it?' There was a creaking noise and I turned to see the other door swing open. The sky through it was blue and clear. Its companion through which I had entered showed the dark night I had walked in from. My body felt rigid, so this was it, I found my head nodding in assent, but my legs now felt like jelly. I took a step it was like wading through deep mud.

'Francis?' Dr Pickles had put on his glasses, I could see his confusion; Carna held his hands. His eyes flicked to the two open doors. She gently turned his face towards her and kissed him on the lips. I felt the pressure around me release. I clutched at the medallion; it gave me strength. It was now or never.

I stepped out into the sunlight.

Lightning Source UK Ltd.
Milton Keynes UK
UKHW021830251118
332965UK00017B/359/P